best

MW01031696

"Time travel, ancient legends, and seductive romance are seamlessly interwoven into one captivating package."
—Publishers Weekly on Midnight's Master

"Dark, sexy, magical. When I want to indulge in a sizzling fantasy adventure, I read Donna Grant."
—Allison Brennan, *New York Times* bestseller

5 Stars! Top Pick! "An absolute must read! From beginning to end, it's an incredible ride."
—Night Owl Reviews

"It's good vs. evil Druid in the next installment of Grant's Dark Warrior series. The stakes get higher as discerning one's true loyalties become harder. Grant's compelling characters and continued presence of previous protagonists are key reasons why these books are so gripping. Another exciting and thrilling chapter!"
—RT Book Reviews on Midnight's Lover

"I definitely recommend Dangerous Highlander, even to skeptics of paranormal romance – you just may fall in love with the MacLeods."
—The Romance Reader

Don't miss these other spellbinding novels by
DONNA GRANT

CHIASSON SERIES
Wild Fever
Wild Dream
Wild Need

DARK KING SERIES
Dark Heat
Darkest Flame
Fire Rising
Burning Desire
Hot Blooded (Dec 30, 2014)
Night's Blaze (Mar 31, 2015)

DARK WARRIOR SERIES
Midnight's Master
Midnight's Lover
Midnight's Seduction
Midnight's Warrior
Midnight's Kiss
Midnight's Captive
Midnight's Temptation
Midnight's Promise
Midnight's Surrender

DARK SWORD SERIES
Dangerous Highlander
Forbidden Highlander
Wicked Highlander
Untamed Highlander
Shadow Highlander
Darkest Highlander

ROGUES OF SCOTLAND SERIES
The Craving
The Hunger (October 13, 2014)

SHIELD SERIES
A Dark Guardian
A Kind of Magic
A Dark Seduction
A Forbidden Temptation
A Warrior's Heart

DRUIDS GLEN SERIES
Highland Mist
Highland Nights
Highland Dawn
Highland Fires
Highland Magic
Dragonfyre

SISTERS OF MAGIC TRILOGY
Shadow Magic
Echoes of Magic
Dangerous Magic

Royal Chronicles Novella Series
Prince of Desire
Prince of Seduction
Prince of Love
Prince of Passion

Wicked Treasures Novella Series
Seized by Passion
Enticed by Ecstasy
Captured by Desire

**And look for more anticipated novels from
Donna Grant**

Burning Desire (Dark Kings)
*The Hunger (*Rogues of Scotland*)
Moon Kissed (LaRue)

coming soon!

WILD
NEED

A CHIASSON STORY

DONNA GRANT

This is a work of fiction. All of the characters, organizations, and events portrayed in this novel are either products of the author's imagination or are used fictitiously.

Wild Need
© 2014 by DL Grant, LLC
Excerpt from *Burning Desire* copyright © 2014 by Donna Grant

Cover design © 2014 by Leah Suttle

ISBN 10: 1942017014
ISBN 13: 978-1942017011

www.DonnaGrant.com

Available in ebook and print editions

PRONUNCIATIONS & GLOSSARY

GLOSSARY:

Andouille (ahn-doo-ee) & **Boudin** (boo-dan)
Two types of Cajun sausage. Andouille is made with pork while boudin with pork and rice.

Bayou (by-you)
A sluggish stream bigger than a creek and smaller than a river

Cajun ('ka-jun)
A person of French-Canadian descent born or living along southern Louisiana.

Etoufee (ay-two-fay)
Tangy tomato-based sauce dish usually made with crawfish or shrimp and rice

Gumbo (gum-bo)
Thick, savory soup with chicken, seafood, sausage, or wild game

Hoodoo (hu-du)

Also known as "conjure" or witchcraft. Thought of as "folk magic" and "superstition". Some say it is the main force against the use of Voodoo.

Jambalaya (jom-bah-LIE-yah)
Highly seasoned mixture of sausage, chicken, or seafood and vegetables, simmered with rice until liquid is absorbed

Maman (muh-mahn)
Term used for grandmother

Parish
A Louisiana state district; equivalent to the word county

Sha (a as in cat)
Term of endearment meaning darling, dear, or sweetheart.

Voodoo (vu-du) – New Orleans
Spiritual folkways originating in the Caribbean. New Orleans Voodoo is separate from other forms (Haitian Vodou and southern Hoodoo). New Orleans Voodoo puts emphasis on Voodoo Queens and Voodoo dolls.

Zydeco (zy-dey-coh)

Accordion-based music originating in Louisiana combined with guitar and violin while combing traditional French melodies with Caribbean and blues influences

PRONUNCIATION:

Arcineaux (are-cen-o)

Chiasson (ch-ay-son)

Davena (dav-E-na)

Delia (d-ee-l-ee-uh)

Delphine (d-eh-l-FEEN)

Dumas (dOO-mah-s)

Lafayette (lah-fai-EHt)

LaRue (l-er-OO)

ACKNOWLEDGEMENTS

A special thanks goes out to my family who lives in the bayous of Louisiana. Those summers I spent there are some of my most precious memories. I also need to send a shout-out to my team – Bridgette B, Candace C, Stephanie D, Kelly M, Kristin N, Vanessa R. You guys are the bomb. Hats off to my editor, Chelle Olson, and cover design extraordinaire, Leah Suttle. Thank you all for helping me get this story out!

Lots of love to my amazing husband, Steve, and my kiddos - Gillian, and Connor. Thanks for putting up with my hectic schedule and for knowing when it was time that I got out of the house. And a special hug for my furbabies Lexi, Sheba, Sassy, Tinkerbell, and Diego.

Last but not least, my readers. You have my eternal gratitude for the amazing support you show me and my books. Y'all rock my world. Stay tuned at the end of this story for the first sneak peek of *Burning Desire*, Dark Kings book 3 out Sepember 30, 2014. Enjoy!

Xoxo
Donna

PROLOGUE

Algiers, Louisiana on the outskirts of New Orleans
Six years earlier...

The clear, cool October night was shattered with screams.

And blood.

Davena stood in horrified fear as she watched her mother being ripped apart in front of her. There was no attacker for her to see, no one to try and save her mother from. There was only...magic.

"I told her," Delia whispered.

Blood coated every inch of their small living room from cut after cut that appeared on their mother. Through the window, Davena could see the cause of all the horror. She was dressed in all white, her midnight skin cast in an orange glow from the flames she brought to life around her.

In all her seventeen years, Davena had never

thought to see her family attacked by Delphine. Her mother kept clear of the Voodoo priestess, so what would make Delphine attack?

Delia grabbed Davena's arm and tried to turn her from the window. "We need to go. Now!"

But Davena couldn't leave. It was their home and their lives being ripped apart. She wiped at a tear and rushed to her mother who now lay still and quiet, her eyes staring blankly up at Davena. She tried to gather her mother against her, but the blood made it impossible to get a hold of her. Davena took her mother's hand instead.

Suddenly, her mother's head turned and her brown eyes locked with Davena. "Run," she whispered with her last breath.

Davena looked up as she heard the crackle of fire. Smoke billowed up from beneath the front door. She quickly covered her head with her arm as all the windows shattered and flames shot high. The fire consumed her mother, and Davena barely got away without being burned. Hands grabbed her from behind and half-dragged, half-carried her into the hall.

Davena looked into her sister's face. Delia's green eyes were wide, and there were tear marks down her cheeks. She had a bag on her shoulder overflowing with clothes. Delia let it drop as she slid down the wall to sit on the floor. "She's not going to let us live. We're going to burn alive, Davena. All the doors are locked with her magic."

They could either remain huddled in fear, or they could fight. Davena was about to head to her room to see about climbing out the window when she remembered her mother had foreseen this day - and a way out.

Davena grabbed Delia's bag. "Get up," she said through the thickening smoke.

Delia coughed, her arm covering her mouth. She climbed to her feet with the help of the wall. "Why?"

"Because we're getting out."

Davena blinked against the smoke stinging her eyes and burning her throat. She desperately wanted to breathe in clean air. Their time was running out. If they didn't hurry, they would never get out.

Fire flared up just as they reached the doorway to their mother's room, as if it knew they were trying to get free. Delia screamed. Davena hastily covered her sister's mouth and put a finger on her lips to urge her to silence.

If Delphine thought they were alive, she wouldn't stop. Ever.

Davena pulled her sister in front of her and then shoved her through the flames. A moment later, she jumped through them herself. The fire singed her skin, the heat crushing. Never in her life had she ever been afraid of anything. Now she was terrified of everything – especially fire.

It destroyed without conscience, killed without consideration. It was judge, jury, and executioner.

And it had its sights set on them.

The room was enveloped with flames. Delia's screams could be heard over the roar of the fire.

Davena didn't try to hush her sister again. The screams would help Delphine think they were dying.

Davena focused on shoving aside the dresser to reveal a small door. She managed to slide it a few inches when the flames suddenly fell back. Hesitating, Davena listened and heard the tell-tale squeak of the front door hinges. Delphine wasn't going to let the flames kill them. She was coming for them herself.

Delia was on the floor coughing uncontrollably. Davena shoved the dresser with all her might, her teeth gritted. Suddenly, the dresser slid against the carpet enough that the small door became visible. She let out a relieved sigh at seeing it. Davena had been a small child when her mother had told her about it, and then never brought it up again. Until that moment, Davena thought she had dreamed it.

But her mother was nothing if not prepared.

With tears stinging her eyes from the smoke and her mother's gruesome death, Davena reached for the handle on the door without thinking. She hissed in a breath as the metal burned her skin. It was all she could do to hold in the scream of pain.

Davena pulled her hand back as some of her skin stuck to the handle. She blinked through her rapidly falling tears. There was no time to see to the wound. She snatched a shirt hanging out of Delia's bag and wrapped it around her hand before she reached for the handle again.

It took three tugs, but the door finally gave and flew outward. Davena glanced inside and saw nothing but cobwebs and a tunnel. It was their only chance at freedom – and life.

She grabbed Delia and shoved her through the door. Her sister landed on her hands and turned her head around to look back. Davena hesitated in the door as the light from the fire illuminated Delia. The terror that found them that night would be with them for the rest of their lives.

That second of hesitation was all Davena allowed them before she stepped into the tunnel and closed the door behind her. They crawled through the tiny, dense space for over fifty feet with no end in sight. The air was oppressive and sweltering, but at least they were no longer in danger of burning to death.

She was glad she couldn't see what was around her, because she was certain it wasn't just the ground that her hands kept touching. Her right hand throbbed in time with her heart from the burn. Later, she would have to see to it, and no doubt it would be impossible to use for a while, as well as scar, but how could she complain about that when she had her life?

Davena didn't know how far they had crawled. The silence was as eerie as the flames. Just when she thought she couldn't go anymore, she heard the faint trickle of water.

"Do you hear that?" Delia whispered.

Davena swallowed hard as she recognized the drainage ditch the tunnel led them to. "We made it."

Delia gave a soft whoop and stood suddenly,

her foot splashing in the water. "We actually did it!"

Davena climbed out of the tunnel and wiped her good hand on her filthy jeans. She and her sister were both covered in sweat and dirt, their faces stained black with smoke, but they were alive. Davena sucked in mouthfuls of clean, fresh air and looked to the night sky that was red-orange with the flames from their home.

"She'll find the tunnel," Delia said and motioned to the tunnel. "You know it."

Davena adjusted the bag on her shoulder. "She'll burn the house until there's nothing but ash. There won't even be bodies to identify."

"I hope you're right. If not, she'll come for us."

"No," Davena said confidently. "We're safe now."

CHAPTER ONE

Crowley, Louisiana
Present day...

Beau Chiasson was tired and hot. The September sun was brutal on the already roasted earth. The summers were always vicious in the bayou, but this past one had been exceedingly so. The thick, ominous rain clouds tempted everyone with the promise of a brief respite from the heat.

He put his truck into park and reached the store just as the first fat drops of rain landed on the windshield. Beau smiled and leaned his head back as he closed his eyes. The sound of the rain was soothing, restful. He didn't know how long he sat there before he opened his eyes and saw the steam rising from the concrete as the rain continued. It was now a steady downpour that would cool the temperatures several degrees.

Out of the corner of his eye, he saw a flash of golden blond, and immediately his gaze snapped in that direction. Instantly, he sat up and focused. Beau could still recall the first time he saw Davena Arcineaux. It had been just a year before, with the same stormy weather. She had swerved to miss a dog running across the road and landed her car in the ditch.

Beau hadn't helped her that day. Others had been quick to reach her before he could. She had stepped out of her car into the mud and was immediately drenched.

He still wasn't sure if it was the uncertainty he saw in her gaze as she looked around, or the take-charge attitude she had as she got her sister out of the car. Either way, there was definitely something appealing and altogether fascinating about her.

Snapping out of his reverie, his gaze followed Davena as she walked laughing in the rain. Most shielded themselves from getting wet, but not Davena. She welcomed it, eyes bright and lips wide. Her head tilted back to let the rain fall on her face. She remained that way for several seconds before she smoothed her hair out of her face and walked to the doors of the veterinary clinic.

Beau could stare at her all day. It was the same every time he saw her. He gave a rueful shake of his head and opened the truck door to step out into the rain. He shut the door and started to walk away when he glanced back at Davena. He paused when her gaze met his. Even from across the street, he knew the exact color of her eyes – spring green.

They were as bright and enchanting as her laugh.

Davena and her sister kept mostly to themselves, just as the Chiassons did, so Beau had yet to actually talk to her. Not that he would. Why bother getting to know her? The Chiasson name would be carried on through Vincent and Lincoln. That was enough for him and Christian. Especially Christian. If anyone was adverse to finding a woman to share life with, it was Christian.

Beau nodded a greeting at Davena before he strode into the store. He tried to forget the way her shirt molded to her breasts, or how her hair looked like spun gold, even wet. He desperately tried to ignore how his body instantly came alive at seeing her.

He grabbed a basket and pulled out his list of the items he needed for dinner. It didn't take him long to get them and start toward the check out. He turned the corner and heard a soft intake of breath right before he collided with someone.

There was a soft, feminine gasp. Immediately, Beau released the basket and grabbed a hold of the person. His hands wrapped around thin arms as he looked down into spring green eyes. He could only stare dumbfounded at Davena. The ends of her blonde hair dripped onto her soaked pink plaid shirt. It was the closest he had ever been to her, and he found it wasn't nearly close enough.

Beau felt a shiver run through her, and even though he knew he should release her, he couldn't. He held her, marveling at her simple beauty.

"I'm sorry," she said, her gaze skating away for a heartbeat. "I wasn't watching where I was going."

He cleared his throat. "It's my fault. I had my head down."

Beau knew he should let go of her, but his fingers refused to loosen their hold. Her skin was warm beneath his palms, and a slight flush stained her cheeks. She was utterly charming without even meaning to be. Beau was thoroughly shocked to discover he wanted to know her, to hear her laugh, to walk with her down the street.

Then he remembered who he was.

He released her and took a step back, instantly missing the feel of her smooth skin. "My apologies."

Beau bent to pick up his basket. He straightened and threw a glance at her over his shoulder. Her guileless eyes watched him. He blew out a breath and started to walk away.

Only to be halted when she said, "I'm Davena Arcineaux. I don't think we've met."

Everything he had learned as a Chiasson, as a protector of the parish, told him to walk away and keep a professional distance. Yet, he found himself turning back to her.

Her oval face with her soft, clear skin was sun-kissed, making her golden locks stand out even more. She tucked her hair behind her ear, giving him a glimpse of her long neck. How he wanted to slide his fingers along the column of her throat and then kiss his way down.

His balls tightened just picturing it in his head. Beau mentally gave himself a shake. "I'm Beau. Beau Chiasson."

"I know," she said with a faint smile.

His gaze locked on her lips. Did she know how appealing she was? Did she have a clue how much he wanted to yank her against him and kiss those luscious lips?

"Everyone knows the Chiassons."

Beau had to get away from her. She was trouble with a capital T. "Is that right?"

"You know it is. I just haven't figured out why everyone all but whispers the Chiasson name."

And there it was. The reason why Beau, like Christian, knew it was better to keep himself apart from any entanglements – no matter how attractive and tempting.

That was the curse of a Chiasson. They kept the bayous safe from supernatural elements, but in turn, they were outcasts. If they dared to marry, it never ended well. Most of the time it was with death – like what happened to his mother.

Still, it didn't stop the ache inside him for someone to share his life with.

"You've been here only a year. I'm sure you'll figure it out soon enough," he said briskly and turned away once more.

The words were like acid on his tongue, but it had been necessary. For himself and the beautiful and tempting Davena. He wasn't sure he could keep his distance. The words, as well as his brisk tone should make Davena rethink getting to know him.

It was what he wanted. Why then did he feel like shit for doing it?

Beau lengthened his strides to the checkout and set his basket down. Waiting for each item to be scanned and packaged felt like an eternity. He hastily tossed down some money and grabbed the bags as he hurriedly walked from the store.

Once inside his truck, he clutched the steering wheel, closed his eyes, and thought of Davena. Her face materialized in his mind, showcasing every detail. Right down to the flecks of gold in her eyes.

He sighed and snapped his eyes open. The sooner he forgot about her the better. Distance was his friend at the moment. Beau started the truck and backed away. He pulled out onto the road heading home, but even with music blaring through the speakers, he could still hear Davena's voice in his head.

~ ~ ~

Davena watched Beau driving away. She hadn't needed anything in the store, and it hadn't been an accident running into him. Well, it had sort of been an accident.

She had been trying to find a way to run into him. Before she knew it, she had been so absorbed in her thoughts of how, that she had done just that. Literally. She had ended up in his arms and looked up into blue eyes so bright and vibrant that it was all she saw. They were penetrating, piercing. It was almost as if he peered into the depths of her soul.

Perhaps it was the whispers around town about the Chiassons that first caught her attention, but once she saw the tall, dark-headed Beau, nothing else mattered. After that, she was always looking for some glimpse of him and hoping that she might get to talk to him one day.

Davena didn't know if it was the secrecy around the Chiasson family, or how others tended to keep their distance from them, but she was curious to know more. It didn't hurt that Beau made her heart skip a beat and her stomach do that fluttery stuff that felt as if she were on a roller coaster.

All of the Chiasson brothers were good looking, but Beau stood out. From what she had seen, he was a little more reserved than the other three brothers. Vincent, the eldest, kept everyone and everything in check. Often by his side was the dark-haired beauty, Olivia. It was rumored that a wedding would soon be coming.

Then there was Lincoln. He was the one who wore the easy smile, the one who was never far from the beautiful flame-haired attorney that had set up a new practice here in town. The love shining between the two was so obvious that Davena wondered why they weren't married yet.

Next up was Christian. He could be seen teasing his family, but with one look, he could stop a person in their tracks. To Davena's knowledge, no woman was attached to either Christian or Beau.

She thought of Beau's deep brown hair with its streaks of bronze from his time in the sun. Her fingers itched to run through the strands, to see if they were as silky as they looked. And the length.

She'd always had a thing for guys with long hair. Beau's came to just below his jaw, giving him a devil-may-care appearance.

"Damn, but he's hot," she mumbled to herself.

Davena turned once his silver truck was out of sight. The lone cashier, a thirty-something woman with dirty blonde hair and dark eyes was staring at her with a look of disapproval.

"You'll stay away from those Chiasson boys if you know what's good for you," she stated with a sneer.

"And why is that?" Davena wanted to know why the entire parish was almost half-scared of the Chiasson family. What was it about them? They looked innocent enough.

"Heed my warning," the woman said. "If you want to stay alive, you'll keep your distance from that family. Even the sister was wise enough to leave."

Sister. Beau had a sister? That was the first Davena had heard of it, but then she had been focused on Beau.

Davena didn't bother to respond to the cashier as she walked back out into the rain. As soon as she returned to the veterinary clinic, Delia looked up from the receptionist desk with irritation.

"What?" she asked.

Delia rolled her eyes. "You know what. You went chasing after a guy. We're supposed to be working."

"And why not?" Davena leaned her forearms on the chest high counter and peered over the side to see what Delia was typing. "We've been safe for a year. Delphine thinks we're dead. Everything is fine, and I haven't shown any interest in a guy, unlike you."

"Fine?"

Davena bit back a sigh at the anger and resentment in her sister's voice. It was the same argument they'd had since the night they had run from their home.

"Nothing is *fine*," Delia stated. "Our mother was murdered, and we didn't even get to go to the funeral. Her killer is running around free as a bird."

"You want to try and stop-" Davena paused to look around the office and then whispered, "Delphine?"

Delia met her gaze. "We could try."

Davena couldn't hold back a laugh. "You're insane. We have nothing to fight against her magic."

The door opened with the next client before Delia could say more in response. Davena hurried to the back, thankful that the conversation was over. She wasn't fool enough to think Delia would drop it entirely, though.

Davena stopped in front of the cages filled with dogs and cats. The dogs, tails wagging, came to the front looking for some attention. Most of the cats remained asleep, while a couple deigned to crack open an eye at her, stretch, and then slip a paw through the bars to get her notice.

She lavished affection on each of them. She had always been partial to animals, so it had been fortunate that a position had been open at the animal clinic. Even more opportune was the fact that the doctor paid her in cash. It had taken a few months, but as soon as the receptionist left, Davena was able to get Delia hired on, as well.

It wasn't that Delia needed someone to watch her all the time, but she didn't always think things through. She wanted revenge for what happened to their mother. So did Davena, but she understood that to go up against a Voodoo priestess as powerful as Delphine meant certain death.

She wasn't ready to die. There was still so much of her life in front of her that may or may not include a husband and a family.

But to Delia, the only thing that mattered was killing Delphine.

With Delia working at the vet's, Davena could watch her somewhat. Her free time was severely cut down, which allowed Davena to sleep better at night, as well.

"Davena!" Delia shouted from the front

She gave the cat she had been petting one more scratch beneath his chin before she returned to her job. Davena opened the door and smiled at the elderly woman with her overweight dog. "Let me get Boomer weighed in," she said and lifted the chunky Maltese.

Even as she spoke soothing words to the dog, Davena couldn't stop her thoughts from drifting to Beau Chiasson with his captivating eyes and gentle touch.

CHAPTER TWO

Beau had just finished chopping the onion and bell pepper and moved on to the garlic when the back door opened and Vincent walked in. Beau glanced up at his eldest brother, noting the smile that was a constant on his face of late.

It hadn't been so long ago that Vincent had thought to live his life alone. Then Olivia returned to Lyons Point, and everything changed.

"It's all set for tonight," Vin said as he pulled out a chair and sat at the table.

Beau nodded. "Which area do I have?"

"I thought we'd all stay together this time."

Beau stopped chopping and turned his head to Vincent. "Since when? We cover more ground when we split up."

"That's a fact, and we've all been pretty lucky in keeping our injuries to a minimum. I think we should be more careful now, though."

"Ah." Beau understood all too well that this was about Olivia and Ava.

Vincent's forehead creased. "What's that supposed to mean?"

"It doesn't mean anything."

"Spit it out, runt." Though Vincent's words were said in jest, his tone had taken a hard note.

Beau set down his knife and faced him. "It means, that you're thinking has shifted from protecting the parish to protecting Olivia, just as Lincoln is now thinking the same about Ava. Don't get me wrong, I like Olivia and Ava, and I understand."

"But," Vin urged.

Beau looked around the kitchen remembering when they were children how they would all pile in there and watch their mother cook while their father readied his weapons for the night.

He swallowed and shoved aside the memory. "But nothing has changed for me, or Christian. The house and land are more protected than any other place for thousands of miles. If you and Linc want to stick close to your women, then do it. I still think we should split up."

"Just last week we killed that swamp monster, and that took all four of us. If we hadn't all been together, it could've killed whoever stumbled upon it."

"I know." Beau watched his brother, waiting to see what he would say next.

Vincent let out a deep breath and placed his hands on the table before he pushed to his feet. "Are you trying to get yourself killed?"

"No. We have a job to do. Isn't that what you

told us when Mom and Dad were killed? Didn't we all step in and do our parts? That's all I'm trying to do now."

"We took risks. Too goddamn many risks!" Vincent shouted. "I don't want to bury another member of my family, Beau. Can't you see that?"

Anger Beau didn't even know had been bubbling within him exploded. "And I don't want any more people to needlessly die like Olivia's parents because we were grouped together over worry that one of us might get hurt!"

"That's enough. Both of you," came Christian's calm voice from the door.

Beau glanced toward the door to find Lincoln standing beside Christian. They walked further into the kitchen with Lincoln leaning against the wall, and Christian moving to the stove to see what was cooking.

Lincoln fingered the hilt of one of his Bowie knives strapped to his leg. "Both of you are right. We tried to tell you that, but the shouting was out of control."

"I'm surprised Olivia and Ava didn't come running in here," Christian said with a chuckle.

Vincent ran a hand through his long, dark hair and sat back down. "I just want to keep the family I have."

"We all do," Lincoln said, his blue eyes briefly meeting Beau's.

Beau turned back around and picked up his knife. He began to dice the garlic and felt Christian's gaze. He shot a glance at his brother and raised a brow. "What?"

"What's really bothering you?"

He wouldn't – couldn't – tell them about Davena. Vincent and Lincoln would encourage him, because if they could find women who understood what they did, then so could he.

The fact was, he wanted them to push him into going to her. It was that and that alone that kept him quiet. Both Olivia's and Ava's life had been in danger, and luckily both Vin and Linc had been able to save them.

But what if they hadn't?

Beau knew it would've completely destroyed both of his brothers. They were strong, determined men, but their hearts belonged to their women. If those women were killed...it would end them.

Their mother's murder had shattered their father. His grief had made him reckless, and that's what got him killed the same night. In one fell swoop, the five Chiasson children had become orphans. Beau told the others he didn't remember much of that night because he had been protecting their sister, Riley, but he remembered every second of it.

Love was so powerful it could do amazing things. Losing that kind of love, however, could obliterate someone as it had their father.

"Beau?" Lincoln called.

He swallowed and moved the diced garlic into the pan with the olive oil and onion to sauté. "I'm fine."

"Bullshit," Christian said.

Vincent's hand hit the table with a slap. "You can't fool us."

"True," Lincoln said. "You might as well tell us. We'll be on your ass until you do."

Beau dumped the chopped chicken breast into the pot. "Any word from our cousins? Was that bitch of a priestess taken care of?"

There was a stretch of silence, and Beau knew that behind him his brothers were looking at each other trying to determine whether to let him change the subject or not.

"Solomon called," Vin said. "They released Delphine after she vowed to leave Ava and Jack alone."

Lincoln gave a shake of his head. "I'm most grateful for that, but they could've had her reverse the curse upon the LaRue line."

"They've been werewolves for so long they probably didn't think it mattered," Christian said.

Beau snorted derisively. "I saw the way Solomon acted with Kane. It matters. They want the curse gone."

"They're making do hunting in and around New Orleans just as we do," Vincent said. "We survive, and so do they."

"Speaking of surviving," Christian said. "Instead of all of us staying together or separating, let's pair up."

Beau stirred the food and let his brothers sort out who was going where. It wasn't long before Ava and Olivia came down and joined the conversation.

It made him cognizant of the fact that so very much had changed. The last time female laughter had been in the house it had been Riley's. God how he missed his sister, but he agreed with Vincent that she needed to be as far from Lyons Point as possible.

Out of all of them, Riley had a chance at a normal life, and all four brothers were going to see that she got it. She made no secret of her anger at not being able to return home, but Vin came up with valid reasons to keep her in Austin as she finished her degree.

"It's odd, isn't it?" Christian said as he leaned against the counter near Beau.

"What's odd?"

"This," Christian said with a jerk of his chin to the table where the two couples sat.

Beau glanced over his shoulder and shrugged. "Mom and Dad would be happy."

"Without a doubt. As much as I like the girls, I think we might want to think of moving out."

Beau met Christian's gaze and nodded. "I've been thinking the same thing lately. I feel like the third wheel most of the time. They want their privacy, and I think they do things because we're around."

"I know they do," Christian replied with a grin. "They'd rather be having sex than watching movies with us."

Beau chuckled and elbowed Christian in the arm. "Both Vin and Linc will argue that we remain. They'll say there are enough rooms."

"There are enough rooms, but that still doesn't make it right."

"Nor does living in sin, as Maria puts it," Beau said, smiling as he thought of Olivia's grandmother.

Christian's smile widened. "Maria is getting her wedding to plan. It's still a few months off yet though."

"I'd just as soon elope than plan something big if it were me." As soon as the words left his mouth, Beau regretted them.

Christian's brow rose as he regarded him. "Is that so? Who are you considering?"

"No one. I was just making a statement."

"You lie for shit, Beau. You've been thinking about it."

He shot Christian a withering look. "Of course I have, dumbass. It's all Olivia and Ava can talk about, and when they aren't talking about it, Vincent and Lincoln are. I bet any day Linc proposes to Ava. Then there will be two weddings being planned."

"Just kill me now," Christian said sarcastically as he dropped his head back to look at the ceiling. "Do you know I couldn't sit down in the media room the other night because of all the wedding magazines and notebooks? There were color swatches everywhere."

"Hell, I didn't even know what a swatch was until Ava brought them to Olivia and patiently explained them to me. In minute detail," Beau said with a sigh.

Christian grunted as he folded his arms across

his chest. "Remember when we didn't have to worry about watching those chick flicks or having room for our beer in the fridge because of their vitamin water?"

Beau wondered if Davena liked beer. Then he grew angry because he shouldn't care what she liked or didn't like. She wasn't part of his life and never would be.

"You're doing it again," Christian said.

"What?"

"Scowling."

Beau opened his mouth to argue the point when he realized he was doing just that. He relaxed his face and concentrated on the meal.

Christian walked to the fridge and pulled out two beers. He opened them and handed one to Beau. "Who is she?"

"There isn't anyone."

"Remember when I said you lie for shit. You're doing that again too."

"Don't you have someone else to bother?"

Christian smiled before he took a long drag of the beer. "Nope. Out with it."

Beau wanted to tell him about Davena. Christian would be the voice of reason, the voice that set him straight on removing her consideration for his future. Yet he didn't.

"I realized today that you were right."

"Holy shit," Christian said and took a step back in mock surprise. "It's only taken twenty-some odd years to hear that from you. As your older brother, I can say I'm proud of you," he said and put his hand on Beau's shoulder.

Beau jerked away from him and frowned. "You're a dick."

"Among other things." Christian took another drink of beer. "What was I right about?"

"Not being...encumbered," Beau said and nodded his head to the table.

"Ah," Christian said, his eyes growing big as realization set in. "Honestly, I was worried that you'd fall in with their thinking."

Beau shook his head. "You don't have to worry about me."

"Is that so? If that's your thinking, why are you so angry? Could it be that there is someone, but you just don't want to give in because you're afraid?"

Beau glared at Christian.

"You're right to be afraid, little brother," Christian said, all the teasing gone from his voice. "Death follows this family close. You bring a woman into the fold, you're ushering her toward a grim reaper."

CHAPTER THREE

Davena sighed in frustration and plopped her head back on the pillow twice, still unable to get comfortable. The rain had been steady for two straight days, putting everyone in an irritable mood. She gave up trying to sleep and opened her eyes. The porch light shining through the blinds only added to her annoyance. It didn't help that it was her night on the couch while Delia got the bed.

Why she ever agreed to that deal, she'd never know? The furnished house had been all they could afford – all they could *still* afford. She had thought they'd share the bed, but Delia had refused, stating they needed their space.

Davena rolled her eyes as she remembered that conversation. It hadn't been a pretty one. Davena had given in because it was the first time Delia had found a place herself. Usually, it was Davena searching for a decent – if not cheap – place for them.

Nothing had been easy since the night their

mother was killed. They had left Algiers with barely thirty dollars in their pocket. It had been Delia's money, which was somehow how she became the one responsible for their finances.

Davena had trusted her, because even though money had been tight, they had eaten and had a roof over their heads through the years. There may not have been nights out at the movies or even to a restaurant, but when fighting for your life, none of that seemed to matter.

She threw an arm over her head as she did a quick calculation of what the two of them had been bringing in together for the past few months from work, minus rent, groceries, and their few bills. That's when she realized they should be sitting pretty well.

They were the best jobs they'd had in years. They were making more money now than they ever had, so why then did Delia tell her they had no money to rent a movie that night?

Davena threw off the blanket and sat up. It was true, Delia had been acting strange lately, but that had been the case ever since they came to the small town. Davena had chalked it up to them not moving on after a few months, but now that she looked back and pieced everything together, it was apparent Delia was up to something.

"Great. Just freaking great," Davena said and ran her hands through her ruler straight hair.

She rose from the couch and padded across the wood floors, careful to walk around the creaky boards, to the closed door of the bedroom. There was no bright light showing through the bottom of the door, but neither was it as dark as it should be with the lights out.

Davena put her ear to the door and heard a faint mumbling. Without a doubt, she knew Delia had lit candles. Her heart rate accelerated as she realized her sister was chanting. And chanting meant magic.

A sound from the front of the house had her spinning around. Goosebumps rose along her arm as her heart pounded against her ribs. There was something outside.

She glanced over her shoulder at the door and briefly considered alerting Delia, until she gathered that it could be Delia summoning something.

"I'm going to stuff one of those candles up your ass, Delia," she whispered to herself.

Davena retraced her steps until she stood before the wide window in the living room. She parted the blinds and saw nothing. A laugh erupted from her as she started to step back.

That's when her gaze caught on a shape across the street dressed all in white.

Davena jerked back, tripping over the coffee table in her haste. A scream lodged in her throat as the world went black.

~ ~ ~

Beau came awake instantly, his body covered in sweat and smoke clogging his throat. He shoved aside the sheet and swung his legs over the side of the bed. For long moments, he sat in the quiet of his room trying to determine what caused him to wake so suddenly with an odd – and persistent – feeling of impending doom.

He ran his hands down his face and glanced at the clock. It wasn't yet dawn. He managed to get only three hours of sleep. There would be no returning to dreamland for him. Whatever woke him, wanted him up for a reason. Beau never doubted the signs his body and mind gave him. They had saved his ass on numerous occasions.

Beau looked out his window to see another gray day ahead. The rain was still as steady as the day before. It had made hunting in the bayous the night before miserable. He rose and took a quick shower, not bothering to shave. He was dressed in jeans, pulling a tee over his head as he walked barefoot down the stairs to the kitchen.

The house was quiet as a tomb, but in a few hours it would be filled with laughter and conversation. It was the silent hours that Beau enjoyed the most. He was usually the first to wake, but the silence wasn't what set him on edge. It was the gnawing, distressing feeling that grew by the minute.

He poured a glass of orange juice and walked to the back door. With a flick of his wrist, he unlocked the door and swung it open. He stood in the doorway, his hand on the jam as he looked out past the screened porch to the bayou beyond.

There was something out there. It was waiting, plotting. The question was, who was it after? The normal consensus would be any of the Chiassons, but this time, Beau thought it could be someone else.

The squeak of a rocker had his gaze jerking to the left to see Maria, her long silver hair pulled back in a bun, slowly rocking, her eyes on the bayou.

"I couldn't sleep," she said. "It woke me."

Beau frowned but remained silent. Maria wasn't just Olivia's grandmother, she had learned how to protect herself and her family by using spells and markings from other cultures. By dabbling into that world, Maria had learned...certain things. He didn't speak as he waited for her to say more. She practiced Hoodoo, and that in itself made her a woman worth listening to.

"It's out there, Beau. It's coming for someone, but I don't know who." She swung her dark gaze to him. "Whatever it is, it's going to touch this family."

"They always do, Maria," he said. "It happens when we hunt them."

She was shaking her head before he finished. "No. It's going to take a life. A Chiasson life unless it's stopped."

Beau glanced up, thinking of his brothers, Olivia, and Ava. Then there was Riley. She might not be in Louisiana, but she was still a Chiasson. "The threat is here only?"

"Yes." Maria's face was lined with worry. "Riley is safe. It's everyone else I'm worried about. Especially my Olivia."

"Vin won't let anything happen to her."

Maria smiled sadly. "He may not be able to stop this force. I don't even know if I can. It's...powerful."

Beau licked his lips and stepped out onto the covered porch. The screen surrounding them kept them from being swarmed by mosquitos. "Is this the first time you've felt something like this?"

"Once before. It was here for a very brief time, and gone before I could try to discover what it was. Now, it appears it's here to stay."

"What kind of creature is it?"

She drew in a deep breath and looked back at the bayou. "There are many types of supernatural things out in the world, Beau Chiasson. Don't narrow your thoughts to a creature."

He finished his OJ and sat in the chair next to her. "What do you think it is?"

"I don't have a clue. Not yet, at least. I've been trying to determine what it is since I woke."

"Olivia is going to have your hide when she discovers you got out in this weather."

Maria laughed softly. "She's the last of my family. She can get angry at me all she wants as long as she lives."

Beau wondered how Vin and Linc were going to take the news. It made him infinitely glad he didn't have a woman to worry about.

No sooner had that thought ran through his head than an image of Davena popped up. He swallowed and turned his head away from Maria. He wished he knew if Davena was safe. It wasn't as if he could call her and check without completely freaking her out.

"I hear there is someone in town asking about you," Maria said.

Beau shrugged. "People are always wanting to know stories about our family."

"Do you have mud in your ears?" she asked testily.

Beau swung his head to her to find her steely gaze on him. He sat back, waiting for her to continue.

"I said you," Maria said. "Who do you think would be asking about you?"

He knew. Davena. Beau didn't so much as whisper her name, but Maria's smile said she knew exactly who it was.

"She's a pretty thing. So is her sister, but Davena is much friendlier than Delia. Grace saw Davena ask several people before she approached Grace."

Beau didn't bother to hide his grimace. Grace and Maria had been best friends since both were young girls. Just as Maria had looked after the Chiasson siblings after their parents' deaths, Grace had done the same. Which meant there was no telling what Grace told Davena.

"Don't worry," Maria said. "Grace didn't tell her much, other than you were single and could use a good woman."

Beau dropped his head back and closed his eyes. Was this what it was like to have grandparents or eccentric aunts who liked to meddle?

Her cold fingers clamped around his wrist, turning his attention to her. Maria's eyes were once more filled with distress. "We have to find out what's here. I can't lose Olivia."

He could see her panic rising. She had tried to change the subject by talking about Davena, but whatever woke the both of them had a strong hold on her.

"You said it would touch this family," Beau said slowly as he thought through all she'd said. "But it isn't after us right now. I gather it will come for us when we try to stop it."

Maria nodded, her eyes blinking quickly. "That's my feelings on it. You've felt it too, haven't you?"

"Yes," he admitted with a slight nod. "It woke me."

"What did you see? What did you feel?"

He briefly closed his eyes and thought back to when he first woke. "I didn't see anything. It was just a feeling of trepidation. Like something ominous was coming. And smoke."

"Smoke?" Maria repeated with a deep frown. "I wish we had time, but I think it's already here."

Beau covered Maria's hand with his. "We'll find it."

"I don't want to worry Olivia."

"Vincent needs to know. So do Lincoln and Christian. I have to tell them so we can start looking for this thing."

Maria released him, pulling her hand from his and sat back with a sigh. "Grace is at my house. My place is more protected than hers. She'll remain with me until this thing is caught and ended."

"You're powerful in your own right, Maria. Don't forget that."

"I'm not forgetting it, but this is more powerful than me and Grace combined."

The fact that Maria wasn't just worried but frightened was telling. "What should I be looking for?"

"Death. And magic."

CHAPTER FOUR

Davena woke on the couch. She blinked and stared at the small TV across from her. She stretched as she rolled onto her back and immediately winced. She stilled, recalling the previous night. Had it all been a dream? It had to be. Otherwise, how would she have gotten back onto the couch? And yet, her shoulder blade was sore.

The coffee table. Her gaze went to the table to see nothing out of order. She remembered tripping over it, she remembered falling, and then...nothing.

Davena slowly sat up and looked around. A glance at the clock hanging on the wall above the TV said it was just after six. The sun couldn't penetrate the thick rain clouds fully, only lightening the room enough for her to see without turning on a lamp.

She shoved her hair out of her face, and had to quickly bite back a yelp of pain. Davena fisted her hands and waited until the worst of it had passed.

Then she rose and walked to the bathroom where she flipped on the light and tilted her head to the side as she carefully moved her hair.

The bump was barely visible on her temple, but the bruising was evident, as was the small cut. There was no blood, nor had she woken up on the floor as she should have.

"What the hell is going on?" she asked her reflection.

Davena braced her hands on the edge of the sink and swallowed past the sudden nausea that threatened, which had nothing to do with her injury. Only one other time had she felt such dread. Less than a week later her mother had been murdered.

She broke out into a cold sweat and began to shake. Gagging, she rushed to the toilet, tears falling as she tried not to be sick.

Their life had been good in Crowley. It was a small city surrounded by even smaller towns. She and Delia were making good money and had remained longer than their customary six months. Davena had thought they were through moving.

Her legs buckled, dropping her to her knees as she rested her cheek against the cool porcelain seat. She didn't know how long she stayed that way before the tears finally dried up and the worst of the nausea passed.

Davena wiped her face and straightened. She was going to have to find some way to tell Delia it was time to get moving. They were only two hours from the Texas border. Perhaps it was time they left Louisiana again. They had spent time in Mississippi and Arkansas. It was always tough to convince Delia to leave Louisiana, but she would do it. Then make sure they never returned.

She climbed to her feet and walked back to the living room. Davena inspected the coffee table to see a chip on one edge. She touched it, and the entire table rocked.

Just as she had thought. She hadn't just tripped, she had broken the thing. Someone had cleaned up the entire incident so she'd think she was losing her mind.

Davena's head turned to the bedroom door. Delia was up to something, but Davena had a hard time believing her sister would allow her to believe she was going insane. Delia was many things, but not manipulative. At least she hadn't been.

She then walked to the front door and checked the locks. All were in place. Same with the back door and all the windows Davena could get to. The bedroom door opened just as she finished checking the window over the kitchen sink. Davena whirled around, her head pounding at the quick action.

"Morning," Delia said with a yawn. She shuffled into the kitchen in her bare feet and clicked on the coffee pot before making her way to the bathroom and turning on the water.

Davena pulled out a chair at the tiny kitchen table that only sat two and dropped her head into her hands. They had two hours before they had to be in to work. That was two hours she had to convince Delia to leave Louisiana.

The smell of the coffee brewing filled the small house. As soon as it finished, Davena poured herself a cup and contemplated what to do. One more day wouldn't hurt them. They could turn in their notices at work and be gone by the next day.

By the time Delia walked out of the bathroom in her robe with a towel wrapped around her head, Davena had it all figured out.

"You're going to be late," Delia said as she poured her coffee with four heaping spoonfuls of sugar.

"Let's leave."

Delia threw her an exasperated look. "Very funny. I thought you were happy here."

"I am. I was. I just think it's time to move on. We've stayed longer than we've ever stayed before."

Delia shrugged and faced her as she blew on her coffee. "It's been six years, sis. Delphine didn't come after us in all that time. She's not going to come after us now because she thinks we're dead."

"Did you pick me up last night after I fell?"

"Pick you up?" Delia's forehead furrowed. "What is going on with you? You fell? Are you all right?"

Davena waved away her words and rose to set her empty cup next to the sink. "Yeah, I'm fine. I'm just getting antsy to leave."

"I'm not going."

"What?" she asked, her head whipping around to her sister. "We've always stayed together."

"It's been six fucking years!"

"Don't say that word. Mom hated it."

"Fuck. Fuck. Fuck!" Delia yelled. "Mom is dead, and I'm an adult. I can say whatever I want."

Davena could only stare after Delia as she stormed away, the door slamming after her. They may not share a bed, but they shared a closet and clothes.

She stomped after her sister, throwing open the door and causing Delia to gasp as she turned from the closet, a shirt in hand. "Finished with your temper tantrum? You'd think you were the younger sister."

"Puh-leeze," Delia said with a roll of her eyes. "Ten months separate us. You think you've got it all under control, but the truth is, you're always grasping at straws. There's no control, Davena, but you've never realized that."

Now she was more confused than ever. "Control? What the hell are you talking about?"

"You want to control every aspect of our lives from where we live to how long we stay somewhere."

"Oh, no you don't." Davena began to shake she was so angry. "I distinctly remember leaving many places behind because you were ready before I was. How many decent places have we left? That one in Mississippi was a good place, and the job at the deli was really good."

Delia barked with laughter and yanked the towel off her head, her wet, dark blonde hair spilling to her shoulders. "Louisiana is our home."

"It's where Delphine lives. God!" she yelled and

glanced helplessly at the ceiling. "You're just like Mom. She knew the threat was there, but she remained, taunting Delphine with it until Delphine killed her. And you want to remain in the same state with a Voodoo priestess who wants us dead?"

"You don't get it do you?"

"Obviously not," she replied sarcastically. "Explain it."

Delia crossed her arms over her chest and cocked her hip out. "I'm going to make Delphine pay for what she did to Mom and what she's put us through these last six years."

Davena shook her head in regret. "What have you done, Delia?"

"Nothing. Yet. But I will. I'll get strong enough, and I'll face Delphine."

Davena put her hand to her forehead and closed her eyes. "Mom didn't teach us any of the spells, because she didn't want us involved."

"I followed her many nights while you were out running around with your friends in New Orleans."

Davena dropped her hand to her side and stared dumbfounded at her sister. "Please no. Mom went out of her way to help those who had been cursed with Voodoo. She began it before we were born, and she tried to get out of it after us. She couldn't. Dad was killed as a warning, which is why she spent many, many years away from it all."

"She helped them in secret," Delia said, a smirk on her face. "Mom told you she was out of it, but she wasn't."

Davena's stomach began to churn again. "I

knew she helped those in deep. It wasn't in her nature to turn away someone suffering."

"The spells she learned while practicing Voodoo are what allowed her to do that," Delia said. "I want to do the same."

"You want to use those spells to kill Delphine. How is that any different than what Delphine did to Mom and Dad? You'll be a murderer."

"I'm following in Mom's footsteps. Someone has to. It isn't going to be you," she said with a scathing look.

Davena was taken aback. "Following in her footsteps, my ass. Mom helped people. She would protect us, and the house, but she never harmed anyone – not even Delphine. How is that doing what Mom did?"

"I'll help people once I kill Delphine."

Davena slapped her hands on her legs in frustration. "Do you hear yourself? Do you even know what you're saying?"

"Yep. I'm saying I'm staying here. You can do whatever you want," Delia said and turned on the blowdryer before putting her back to her.

Davena gave up and went to take her shower. The entire time she was bathing, the bad feeling festered in her belly until she was sick with it. There wasn't another word shared between her and Delia the rest of the morning, or on the drive into work. Delia opened the car door before the vehicle was in park and jumped out, practically bounding into work with a bright smile.

Davena shut off the engine and remained in the

car. Her mood matched the gray sky. It was Friday, which meant they closed up at two. Hopefully by then she could decide what to do.

The thought of leaving Delia behind didn't seem right, and yet she knew they couldn't remain in Crowley. Something bad was going to happen, of that Davena was certain.

She had ignored the warnings until the last minute before, and then her mother had pushed her words aside. Hours later, their mother was dead, and they were running for their lives.

Davena looked down at her right hand where the skin was puckered on her palm from the burn she sustained while trying to get the door opened. The scar ran horizontally across her palm, a constant reminder of how quickly life could be changed.

She was so tired of trying to keep going. So many times she wanted to fall down and curl up in a ball, to pretend that life didn't suck major moose dick. The fact was, life did suck the big one.

Not once had she allowed herself to fall apart. That had been Delia, and one of them had to stay strong. Only once had she come close to loosing it. Somehow, she had pulled herself together and carried on. Had it not been for Delia, Davena knew she would've never made it as far as she had. It was her sister that kept her focused.

She wanted to believe that Delia was right and that six years were long enough for Delphine to forget them. But Davena knew how vengeful the priestess could be. She had seen the evidence when the people would come to her mom for help.

It would be a cold day in Hell before Delphine ever forgot them.

CHAPTER FIVE

The hush that fell around the kitchen table was deafening. Beau let Maria do all the explaining of what was going on. He didn't volunteer what he had experienced that morning yet.

Vincent put his arm on the back of Olivia's chair and touched her as he looked at Maria. "And you have no idea what it could be?"

"No," Maria said.

Lincoln rubbed his forehead, his face already lined with worry. "We need it narrowed down some. Is it a ghost? A demon? A creature?"

Maria slid her dark gaze to Lincoln. "How many times do you know what you'll be hunting when you leave this house?"

"Maman's right," Olivia said. "It doesn't matter what it is. It's just another supernatural problem we have to solve."

"We?" Vin said with a raise of his brows. "Oh no, sweetheart. It's a problem my brothers and I have. You and Ava aren't going to leave this house."

Ava lifted her amber gaze to Lincoln. "I thought the entire Chiasson property was warded and protected like the house."

"It is," Lincoln said as he took hold of her hand and squeezed it. "The house is safe. We need y'all to remain inside."

"Don't leave unless one of us tells you to," Vincent told Olivia.

She rolled her eyes. "Oh, come on, babe. You've got to let that go. I thought Maman was in the hospital. How was I to know that creep was responsible for all those deaths?"

"That's the point," Christian said as he leaned back in his chair. "The only people you can trust are in this house."

Beau watched the way the two couples looked at each other before he turned his head away. If his brothers didn't have Olivia and Ava, they would be facing the growing threat differently. They would be heading out now to look for it, not worrying about whether the girls were safe.

Like he was worrying about Davena.

He looked back at the group to find Christian's gaze on him. Beau shoved his hair out of his face and got to his feet. "The women will be safe here. Let's get out there and find whatever this is."

"Night is the best time for hunting," Christian said.

Lincoln grunted. "Most of the time, but if it's a human we're after, we can find them in the day."

Maria pushed the chair away from the table and

stood. She walked to her purse and reached for her keys when Olivia rose so quickly she knocked her chair over.

"Maman, where are you going?"

Maria smiled softly. "Back to my house. As I said earlier, Grace is waiting for me."

"Vincent can bring Grace here. Make Maman stay, Vin."

Vincent stood beside Olivia and pulled her against his side. "Your grandmother is a grown woman. I can't make her stay."

"Damn right," Maria mumbled, the smile gone.

Olivia jerked her head to Vincent. "But you can make me stay?"

"We both will," Maria stated in a no-nonsense voice.

Olivia harrumphed and flattened her lips as she glared at her grandmother.

Maria gave a small nod. "Now that that's settled, I'll expect to hear from y'all later. Grace and I will remain at the house, safely ensconced inside."

She then opened her arms, and Olivia flew into them. They shared a lasting embrace before Maria turned to Ava. Ava hugged Maria tightly, soft words falling from Maria's lips.

Beau and Christian remained behind as the two couples walked Maria to her vehicle. It was still raining, though the rain had diminished to a drizzle.

"I'm going to take a drive around to see if I can find anything. Want to tag along?" Christian asked.

Beau knew the driving would eventually take

them into Crowley. That would put him too close to Davena for his peace of mind. "I'll pass."

"I don't know who you're trying to stay away from, but it won't work. It never does."

"Don't have a clue what you're talking about," Beau said as he pushed open the screen door and walked off the porch.

It didn't matter that he was getting wet. He had spent the last few days soaked, and today wouldn't be any different. Beau looped his thumbs in his belt loops and gazed out over the bayou.

No matter how he tried, he couldn't determine what the threat was. More unsettling, was the fact that he had felt something. Maria sensing something he could understand since she practiced Hoodoo, but not him.

"Thank goodness Maria knows Hoodoo, huh?" Lincoln said as he came to stand beside him.

Beau nodded. Voodoo was a religion, but Hoodoo was a practice of magic that combined some elements of Voodoo. There were instances where Hoodoo was used to combat Voodoo curses. Sometimes they worked. Sometimes they didn't.

"Voodoo isn't to be trifled with," Lincoln said and pulled his long hair back at the base of his neck before he wrapped a piece of leather around it and tied it off.

Beau swept his arm across their view. "We live in Louisiana, Linc. That's like saying a gator shouldn't be teased. It's common sense, even for those who don't live near those practicing the religion."

"Ah, but we've both seen how the Voodoo religion has profited from tourists while we've been in New Orleans. They sell spells, Voodoo dolls, and anything else they can think of."

"I know." Beau had never cared to be near those shops. Some sold fake items, but there were a handful of stores that sold the real things.

Lincoln crossed his arms over his chest and blew out a long breath. "You've been peculiar all morning. Want to tell me what's going on?"

"No." Beau dropped his chin to his chest and kicked at the wet grass. "Maria wasn't the only one who felt something."

There was a heartbeat of silence before Lincoln pushed at his shoulder so they faced each other. "What the hell? And you didn't say anything?"

"Why?" Beau said with a shrug. "Maria's explanation was good enough. There was no need to add mine."

"Did Christian hit you and addle your brains? Of course there's a need," Lincoln said peevishly. Then he mumbled, "Damn fool."

Beau rolled his eyes. As the youngest of the brothers, he was constantly being picked on. Not even Riley was teased as mercilessly as he was, and she was the youngest of them all. But she was the only girl, and for some reason that made her different.

"Enough of that shit," Beau said, his patience at an end.

Lincoln threw up his hands. "Fine, but you're

going to tell me everything."

"There isn't much to tell. I woke up with a feeling of dread twisting my stomach. I came downstairs and found Maria."

Lincoln gave a shake of his head and looked at the house. "Beau, not a single Chiasson has ever had those kinds of things happen to them. We aren't psychics or seers or anything of the sort."

"I know," Beau said wearily. It wasn't anything he hadn't already told himself, but there was no doubt in what he had felt – was still feeling.

"For both you and Maria to feel something..." Lincoln trailed off and hung his head as he put his hands on his hips. "We need to be extra careful. I'm worried like I've never been worried before."

"Ava and Olivia will be safe. We'll remain in two groups to watch each other's back. Christian wants to drive around. I'm going to go out into the bayou."

"I'll go with you," Lincoln said and lifted his head. "We live dangerously every day, but I get the feeling that whatever is here is infinitely more treacherous."

"It's not after us right now, but based on what Maria sensed, we'll find it and get in its way."

Lincoln snorted. "That's when it'll come for us."

"Yeah," Beau said weakly.

Lincoln faced the house as Vincent and Christian joined them. "The Chiasson land has always been a refuge against the things we hunt."

"Your point?" Vin asked.

Beau knew what Lincoln was going to say, and he knew how much it was going to cost both of his brothers.

"Aww shit," Christian mumbled and slapped his hand on his leg.

Linc cleared his throat. "If Maria is right and this thing does come after us, I won't lead it back to Ava or Olivia. I don't want any of us to return here once we figure out what it is."

Vincent opened his mouth to argue, and then stopped. He briefly squeezed his eyes closed and nodded. "You think it's that powerful?"

Lincoln glanced at Beau. "I do. Beau felt something, as well. It was enough to hear it from Maria, but Beau too? I don't want to take any chances, no matter how well we think the house and land are warded."

"Before y'all jump my ass, there was no need to tell you anything. Maria's senses were more targeted than my ominous feeling," Beau explained.

"Shit for brains," Christian said with a wry twist of his lips.

Vin scowled. "I don't care what you thought. You should've told us."

"He's done it now," Lincoln said. "Let's leave it and move on to the next step. I'm going to head out into the bayou with Beau."

Christian scrubbed a hand along the top of his head to ruffle his short dark locks. "I'm going to drive around."

"I'll join you then," Vin said. "We remain together. We don't normally take our cell phones out on hunts, but I think we need to this time. Keep them on vibrate, but at least we'll be able to get ahold of each other if necessary."

Beau gave a nod. "Agreed."

"One more thing," Linc said. "We don't tell the girls we might not be coming back until this is over."

Vin made a sound at the back of his throat. "You don't have to tell me twice. I'd rather explain to Olivia after it's all over than argue with her now. Besides, we might not find anything today."

Christian slapped Vincent on the back. "Better you than me, bro."

Lincoln shoved Christian, causing him to slip on the slight incline leading up to the house. With the wet grass, he went face down with a loud grunt.

Vincent kicked Christian's legs out from underneath him when he tried to get to his feet. Beau joined in the laughter, and waited until Christian was up on his hands before he pushed down on Christian's back, causing him to face plant again.

"I'm going to kick y'all's asses!" Christian bellowed.

The three ran to the house with Christian right on their heels. To some, it might seem odd for them to be joking around when circumstances were so dire, but they had to relieve their emotions somehow so they could face the danger.

They came to a screeching halt in the kitchen when they found all their weapons laid out on the table with the girls packing food and provisions.

Vincent and Lincoln went to their women while Christian kicked off his muddy boots and headed upstairs to change. That left Beau once more unsure of where he stood or what he wanted.

He didn't want the added weight of someone else to watch over and worry about. His family was more than enough. Nor did he want to anxiously await the day his wife would be taken from him in the most heinous way.

In that regard, he wholeheartedly sided with Christian.

Yet no amount of rational thought could stop the need to share his life with someone. To curl up in bed with a woman, and talk about the day or the future. To wake up with her every morning in amazement that someone had chosen him.

As he watched his brothers sharing whispered words with their women, Beau wanted it more than ever.

And he knew who he wanted – Davena.

CHAPTER SIX

Beau stood knee deep in the bayou and wiped the sweat from his brow with the back of his hand. The rain halted an hour into their search of the bayou. With the clouds moving fast, the sun was baking them, making the heat oppressive.

He started forward when he caught sight of a snapping turtle swimming across his path. It was a big one, measuring nearly two feet long. Once the turtle was past, Beau continued onward. Lincoln was off to his left searching, and unfortunately, nothing had been found by either of them in the four hours they had been out.

Every few minutes, Beau cursed himself for not going into town with Christian. He might have caught a glimpse of Davena, which would have calmed him some. Maybe. Hell, he wasn't sure of anything anymore. Not since that encounter with her. She was on his mind constantly, and that could get him killed in his line of work.

He didn't know how Vin and Linc did it. It

might help his brothers knowing their women were safe on Chiasson land. He didn't have that. Davena was out in town with danger closing in.

If they only knew who they needed to protect.

It would also help if they knew *what* they were after.

The crickets were singing loudly, as were the birds. All the animals of the bayou were out in the sunshine after days of rain.

He worked his way forward searching for the tiniest hint of paranormal. It wasn't easy in the murky water, and the longer he went without discovering anything, the more frustrated he became.

Lincoln let out a three-tone whistle. Beau jerked his head to his brother and saw Linc motion him toward an outcropping of land. Beau didn't need to be told twice. He waded forward, careful of where he placed his feet. Lincoln was already there when he stepped out of the water.

Lincoln pulled off his rubber boots and wiggled his toes. "My toes are going to become webbed if we keep this up."

Beau chuckled and sank down on a fallen log next to his brother and removed the pack from his back. He pulled off one boot, then the next before he yanked off his wet socks and slapped them on the tree next to him. "Tell me about it."

"At least the girls packed us extra socks." Lincoln shook his head as he laughed. "Extra socks. Do you know how many times I walked around all day with wet ones?"

"Yep. All our lives."

"Exactly, but what does my Ava think of? Dry socks." Lincoln looked up at the sun and closed his eyes. "How is it that women think of those things, but we don't?"

"You're the one with a woman. You should know."

Beau knew it was the wrong thing to say the moment Lincoln looked at him with his penetrating gaze. Beau wanted to groan in annoyance. He might have gotten away with saying that to Vincent, but Linc looked deeper, listened harder, saw more.

Lincoln rubbed his chin silently for a moment. "Are you really going to follow Christian in his absurd quest to remain alone?"

"Why not? You and Vin have everything covered. Both of you will have children to carry on the Chiasson name."

"Do you really think that's what our parents wanted? Just for two of their children to carry on?"

Beau shrugged and dug his toes into the damp earth. "Riley will also have children. Fortunately, she and her offspring will be far away from this life."

"You won't hear me arguing about that." Lincoln leaned his forearms on his knees. "But do you really want to be alone? Don't think about what we do or how we live. You're talking about spending decades by yourself instead of with someone else."

"I can't think about a future without

considering what we do and how we live. We didn't even have normal high school years, Linc. Not a single one of us went to college, except for Riley, and only because we forced her to go. What kind of normal is there for us?"

"Are you worried about a woman accepting what you do? Ava and Olivia understand things."

Beau sighed and shook his head. "Olivia grew up here. She had already heard the stories about our family, and she knew we were different. Ava, damn, Linc. You were fortunate there. She was born here, and her father was already in our line of work."

"You're a fool if you think that made things easier," Lincoln said with a wry twist of his lips.

Beau shrugged and watched as a young crane tried to fly, only to land awkwardly on a branch just a foot above the water. A moment later, a gator sprang up out of the bayou, his jaws snapping around the crane before he fell back into the water.

"It's not that I want to be alone," Beau finally said. "It's just...I don't want a woman to see how we live. I don't want to have to justify things, or talk her into this way of life."

"If she loves you, it won't matter."

"Bullshit. It matters. You think Ava likes you going out every night? You think she likes the worry involved, wondering which night you'll come home badly wounded? Or if you'll die."

"That's life, Beau. Anyone's life. You think it's any different for those who commute into work? Each time they get into a vehicle could be their last."

Beau gave him a droll look. "You're actually going to compare driving to what we do?"

"No." Lincoln made a sound at the back of his throat, his forehead furrowed and his eyes filled with growing anger. "You know I'm not. I'm trying to prove a point that life itself is full of dangers. You think the innocents that die around here don't know there is danger out in the world?"

"I know."

"Do you really, little brother, because I'm not so sure. If there's someone you want, go get her. You deserve happiness. Hell, we all do. It took me a long time to realize that."

Beau unzipped his pack and pulled out a bottle of water. He drank deeply before he glanced at Lincoln. "I know I won't survive having someone taken from me the way Mom was taken from Dad."

"Who says that's going to happen?"

"The odds are stacked against us with our lifestyle. You can't expect to keep Ava locked in the house all the time. And what about your children? They're going to want to get out and see friends. How are you going to protect them?"

"Mom and Dad protected us. I'll do the same."

Beau had no doubt Lincoln would go to extremes for his family. Any of them would. "I know you mean well, but when faced with what we do, it's better that I remain alone."

Lincoln took a sandwich out of his pack and unwrapped it before taking a bite. "One day you'll find someone who will change your mind," he said around the food.

Beau didn't bother telling him that had already happened.

~ ~ ~

Christian pulled the truck to a stop and turned off the ignition. He sat with his hands on the steering wheel, his gaze out the windshield.

"What's going on?" Vincent asked from the passenger seat.

"I think someone has caught Beau's interest. I thought he might want to come into town with me, but he was quick to decline. Too damn quick."

Vincent opened the door to let in some air and turned his head to Christian. "He was acting peculiar this morning. I chalked it up to him waking with that odd feeling."

"It's more than that. He won't admit it, but I think there's someone."

"Who?"

"That's the question. Let's take a walk around Crowley and see who we run into that could be a candidate."

Vincent laughed. "He's so going to kick your ass when he finds out."

"Don't you mean our asses?" Christian asked as he got out of the truck and shut the door.

"Hey," Vincent said with his hands raised as he came around the back of the truck. "I'm just along for the ride."

"Yeah. No one around here believes that shit," Christian said, lacing his words with heavy sarcasm.

Vincent playfully shoved him as they walked down the street. The smile Christian wore faded as he looked around with his trained eye. The usually smiling, friendly folks kept their gaze on the ground and their footsteps quick as they went about their business.

"I was really hoping Maria and Beau were wrong," Vin said from beside him as they came to a stop. "But from what I'm seeing, there's no doubt something is stirring."

"There's only one reason for people to change so suddenly."

Vin ran his hands through his long hair. "Yeah. Evil. They may not recognize who it is or where it's coming from, but they sense it."

"Most of what we hunt never affects any of the people unless they're targeted. It looks like Maria had cause to be afraid."

Vincent nudged him and walked a little further down the street. They encountered short tempers, rude stares, and hateful words.

"Vampire?" Vincent asked.

Christian shook his head. "People sense them, but it doesn't cause them to act like this."

"A demon could."

"Yep, except I've not seen anything else to point to a demon or possession. It could be a poltergeist."

Vincent gave a rueful shake of his head. "In a small town like this? We would've already heard about it."

"Why do I get the feeling this is going to be something we've not tangled with before?" Christian asked.

"It may call for some time pouring over the Chiasson journal."

Christian nodded a greeting at an elderly couple as they passed. The journal was a record of every supernatural being the Chiasson family had ever encountered, its strengths, its weaknesses, its habitat, and how to kill it.

As a young child, Christian had often snuck downstairs and poured over the journal with a flashlight under his father's desk. A large portion of it had kept him up many nights afterward, afraid to go to sleep.

It wasn't every child that grew up knowing there really could be monsters under the bed. The only thing that did get him to sleep was knowing that nothing could ever penetrate the house and get him or his siblings while they were inside.

"I'd hoped having a look around would give us some kind of clue. We've driven for hours down dirt roads and rice fields, and there are only so many times you can drive up and down the roads in Crowley before someone gets suspicious."

Vincent reached a corner and waited for the stoplight to turn red before he crossed the street. Christian was beside him, his curiosity spiked as to what might have caught his brother's attention.

Then he realized the reason when Vincent walked to the small office Ava used for her law practice. Vincent unlocked the door and strode inside. It took the two of them just a moment to do a quick search to make sure no one had been there.

"What did you think to find?" Christian asked.

Vin shrugged and fiddled with the keys. "Nothing. I just wanted a look around. Lincoln would've come here first."

"Yeah, he would've," Christian said with a nod. "Ava can remotely access her computer here, so I've no doubt she's working from the house."

Vin looked around once more. "Let's head out and see if Linc and Beau found anything."

Beau was the first out of the office. He turned and watched Vincent lock up. "Since we've not heard from either of them, I'm betting they came up as empty-handed as us."

"Most likely," Vincent said and pocketed the keys.

They turned as one, and Beau's gaze snagged on a woman with straight blond hair that just skimmed her shoulders. She got into an old Dodge car and drove off.

"What is it?" Vin asked.

"The town's newest occupants. We might want to look into them. There were two sisters that moved into Crowley about a year ago," he said.

Vin shrugged. "We do occasionally get people who actually want to move into the parish. Crowley is a decent city and very close to all the smaller towns."

"Whatever," he said and waved away Vincent's words. "What do we know about the sisters?"

CHAPTER SEVEN

"Have you lost your damned mind?" Lincoln asked Christian. "Those two sisters aren't the newest people to move into the area. What about that weird family who bought the old Richard rice farm? If you want to look into anyone, that's who I place my vote for. Have you seen their two kids?" Lincoln shuddered. "Right out of a Stephen King novel."

Beau looked around the table at the empty dishes pushed aside from the evening meal as they talked. Just as Vincent had predicted, they had found nothing during their search. Beau had yet to say anything, but what was there to say? He also wanted to know more about the Arcineaux sisters. The fact that it had nothing to do with whatever they were hunting didn't need to be stated.

"Fine," Christian said. "We look into everyone new."

Olivia set down her glass of lemonade. "Need I remind you, Christian, that it wasn't a new member of the area that killed your parents or those women a few months ago? It wasn't new people who came after me, either."

"She's got a point," Vincent said.

Christian looked away from the table. "We can't look into everyone."

"No," Ava said. "Trust your instincts. If the sisters and that family stand out, then look into them both. There's no reason Olivia and I can't do some digging. We're pretty handy with computers."

Olivia's eyes brightened. "Yes! I need something to do."

"Beau?" Vincent said. "What are your thoughts?"

Beau threw up his hands and then let them fall to his thighs. "Ava's idea sounds like a good one."

"You don't have an opinion?" Christian asked with a roll of his eyes. "There's something wrong."

"Nothing's wrong," Beau hurried to say.

Lincoln's blue gaze was once more on him, and no matter how hard he tried, Beau couldn't hold it. Beau pushed his chair back and walked to the fridge. He pulled out a bowl and set it on the table in front of everyone. "I made banana pudding for dessert."

He walked out of the kitchen and straight into the office. He sat behind the desk and opened the laptop. Once his fingers were on the keyboard, however, he couldn't manage to type anything. It seemed wrong for him to dig into Davena's past. She hadn't done anything amiss in her time in Crowley, but there was no doubt he would find something if he looked. Everyone had something in their past they regretted and wanted forgotten.

If he went searching, he *would* find something. What if it was something that led the others to believe she and her sister were the ones in danger? What if he told Davena what he did, and they were wrong about her and her sister? What if the Arcineaux sisters weren't, in fact, the ones being targeted?

What if she decided she never wanted to have anything to do with him?

Beau's phone vibrated in an S.O.S. signal. It was Riley's code that she had programmed in all four of their phones so they would always know when she called.

"Hey, squirt," Beau answered.

"Hey!"

He sat back, instantly on alert at the false happiness in her voice. "What's up?"

"Apparently not my boobs," she said sarcastically. "Do you know they don't stay perky all that long."

"Riley," he said with a sigh. "I don't need to know about that stuff."

"Who else do I talk to about it? It's not as if I have sisters," she complained.

He pinched the bridge of his nose with his thumb and forefinger. "You're about to get a sister-in-law in Olivia, and I don't think it'll be much longer before you can call Ava that, as well."

"I know, and I adore both of them. We talk almost every day."

Beau's eyes snapped open. He knew without

asking that neither Lincoln nor Vincent knew how often Riley and their women spoke. Riley had always been outnumbered in their family, but suddenly, her side was gaining.

She laughed through the phone. "Now that's got you worried, doesn't it."

He stretched out his legs and crossed them at the ankle. "You didn't call to talk about your boobs or to shock me."

"I sure didn't. Damn, but you're perceptive."

Beau couldn't help but smile. Since he and Riley had been the youngest, they got left together a lot. It had brought them closer, and if there was ever a problem, she normally came to Beau first.

"You might as well just tell me instead of hem-hawing around."

Instead of the loud, dramatic sigh he was expecting, there was silence. A thread of fear raced through him.

"You aren't in trouble are you?"

"No, no," she hurried to answer. "I want to come home."

He almost wished she were in trouble. It would be easier to handle than telling her she couldn't come home. "Your deal with Vincent was that you remain in Austin and get your degree from the University of Texas."

"LSU is closer. Can't I transfer there?"

"Look, squirt, you know I want you home. You also know why we all agreed to send you away."

"It's not fair, Beau. I'm a grown woman. I can make my own decisions."

This was what they had all dreaded. When Riley told them to kiss off and did what she wanted. Beau knew it would one day come, but Vincent believed Riley would do what he wanted for the sake of the family.

"Finish the semester-"

"I'm finished with my summer classes," she interrupted.

Beau looked at the computer screen, the cursor waiting for him to type in his search. "Finish the fall semester. I'll convince Vin to let you come home for Christmas, and we can talk to him then."

"Thanks, Beau."

He frowned when he heard the sadness in her voice. "Is it really so bad up there?"

"I've got friends. I've even gone on a few dates. Austin is nice, but it isn't home."

"Be safe, squirt. You know we love you."

"Love ya, too," she said and ended the call.

Beau set aside the phone and sat up, ready to type in his search when his gaze landed on all three of his brothers in the doorway. His gaze shifted to the couch as Ava and Olivia waved at him. When had they all come into the office? Was he that preoccupied with Davena and Riley that he hadn't noticed?

He really was going to have to get his own place. He desperately needed his own time.

"How is Riley?" Christian asked.

Beau met Vincent's gaze. "She wants to come home."

"We gathered that," Vin said tightly.

Lincoln walked into the office and sank into the chair near the desk. "I think her coming home for Christmas is a great idea. It's been a few years since we've seen her."

"Which I warned you wasn't a good idea," Beau added. "I told you to let her return on her breaks, Vin."

"It's for her own good," Vincent said.

Olivia raised a brow at him. "Careful, babe. That might come back on you soon."

Beau narrowed his gaze on the girls who exchanged a look. They knew something. He would bet his LP collection on it. With as often as they spoke with Riley, no doubt all three had formed some kind of plan.

He bit back a smile. Beau really couldn't wait to see how everything all played out. No doubt it would be a doozy for sure.

"I thought y'all were eating dessert," Beau said.

Lincoln shrugged. "We figured you were doing some research, so we thought we'd come and help."

That was the thickest load of crap Beau had ever heard. If he weren't careful, they would discover his interests lay with one Davena Arcineaux.

"What did you find?" Christian asked.

Beau glanced at the blank screen. "I haven't even started."

"I have," Ava said.

Every eye in the room focused on her. She pushed up her reading glasses and adjusted herself on the couch. "I typed in Delia Arcineaux and found an obituary for six years ago."

"Where?" Vincent asked.

Ava glanced up. "A small town called Algiers right outside of New Orleans."

"That means nothing," Christian said. "It's common for criminals to find names in obits and use them."

"Is it common for Davena Arcineaux to have an obituary on the same day? To have died the same day as her sister?" Ava asked.

Beau felt that knot in his stomach tighten. "How did they die?"

Ava pulled off her glasses and looked up at him. "A fire. The mother, Babette Arcineaux, was suspected of being killed in the same fire."

Fire. There had been smoke in his dream. Or at least he had thought he smelled smoke when he woke.

"There's no mother with them," Olivia said.

Lincoln shifted lower in the chair. "It could be just like Christian said. Two women looking for a change of pace find an obituary with the names of two young sisters and take them."

Ava set her glasses aside on the couch. "Except that Davena was seventeen at the time, and Delia eighteen when they died. That matches the Davena and Delia here."

"Were there only three bodies found in the burned house?" Vincent asked.

"There were no bodies," Ava said. "The fire was so intense there was nothing left to identify.

The house was reduced to ashes. When the girls and the mother weren't located, everyone assumed they were in the house."

"What if they weren't?" Olivia said.

Christian walked to the fireplace and put his back to the mantel. "You mean, what if they weren't ever in the house? Why not just tell the authorities where they were?"

"Because they couldn't," Beau said.

Silence lengthened, each lost in thought.

It was Lincoln who broke the quiet. "Has the mother been seen?"

Ava put her glasses back on and punched the keyboard some more. Another ten minutes went by before she gave a shake of her head. "Nothing. None of her credit cards have been used, and no money has been withdrawn from her bank account."

"The mother could've been in the house," Olivia. "She might really be dead."

Vincent walked to the couch and sat on the arm next to Olivia. "It's a possibility."

"That leaves the only reason the girls wouldn't step forward to let others know they weren't dead. They're running from someone," Christian said.

"Or some*thing*," Beau added.

Lincoln sat up and leaned forward. "Ava, do a search on that new family now. Last name Dumas. Father's name is Frank, mother's is Liz."

While everyone was focused on Ava, Beau quietly punched in Davena's name and New Orleans and searched. In a blink, links and photos popped up on the page.

Staring at him was a photo of Davena her freshman year of high school in a cheerleader uniform at a football game. Her green eyes were clear and innocent, and though the ones he had looked into a few days ago were older and warier, they were still the same eyes that matched the same smile, and the same golden hair.

She and her sister hadn't stolen the names. They were Davena and Delia Arcineaux. He suddenly wanted to know what they were hiding from? More than anything, he wanted to be the one to help her.

Idiot. You want to save her so you can bring her into your life and the Chiasson family business? She's better off left on her own.

There was no denying the truth of it. He would help her if she and her sister were the ones in danger, but he would keep his distance.

"There's no record of Frank and Liz Dumas or their children anywhere," Ava said. She looked up at all of them. "They seem to have appeared out of thin air."

Christian crossed his arms over his chest. "Witness Protection Program, perhaps?"

"As if," Lincoln said. "We found our culprits. The Arcineaux sisters are intriguing, but it's the Dumas family we need to dig deeper on."

"I agree," Vincent set.

Christian rolled his eyes. "Fine."

Beau exited his search and shut the laptop. "Where do we start?"

CHAPTER EIGHT

Davena sat against the headboard with her knees hugging her chest. Delia hadn't said two words to her the entire day, and no matter how she tried, Delia wouldn't relent. If anyone should be upset, it should be her, not Delia. Davena glanced over the side of the bed to where her bag was packed. Everything she owned was in that bag.

If asked six years ago if she could live without her iPod, makeup, clothes, and dozens of friends, she'd have said never. After that one life-changing night, she discovered what the important things were.

It wasn't makeup, hairstyles, or clothes. It was money and food and having a safe place to rest her head. She had gone from wearing designer clothes to digging through restaurant garbage for food.

Her iPod, laptop, and even her cell phone were forgotten. No longer did she spend twenty dollars on one meal. Instead, she and Delia made twenty last several days between the two of them.

It brought home what the essentials where – and what was wasteful. Did she often dream of walking into a mall and spending the day shopping? Often. She knew her clothes weren't the latest styles, but they were clean and in good condition. It was a rare event when she and Delia would stop off at Goodwill and rummage through the clothes others had so easily discarded – some still with price tags on them.

Makeup was an indulgent extravagance she only allowed herself a small portion of. Blush, eyeliner, and mascara. As for her hair, there wasn't much she could do with it anyway.

She used to spend hours trying to get it to curl, spending her mother's money on products and tools to get just the right hairstyle. Now, Davena let it go to its natural state – board straight.

A sigh escaped as she rested her chin on her knees. Her body vibrated with the need to leave the area, but she couldn't seem to make herself walk away from her sister. As angry as Delia made her more often than not, they were the only family each of them had.

Leave? She couldn't do it. Whatever might be coming for them, they would face it together.

Davena lifted the covers and settled on her back. Her gaze locked on the ceiling, but it wasn't the square tiles she saw, it was bright blue eyes and chin length dark hair.

"Beau Chiasson," she whispered.

She discreetly asked around about the Chiassons, trying not to let anyone know it was

Beau she was interested in. Somehow everyone seemed to know. If they didn't outright guess it was Beau, they made it clear that Vincent and Lincoln were taken.

What was really odd was how they were so protective of the Chiassons, and yet, they seemed to fear them, as well. It reminded Davena of how the people of Algiers had treated her mother.

At least there was no fear of the Chiassons practicing Voodoo or Hoodoo. That thought brought a smile to her face. They may still be in the bayous of Louisiana, but there was no one attempting Voodoo in Crowley.

Davena touched the wound on her head. It was still tender, the bruise turning a nasty shade of blue-black. The smile disappeared as she remembered what had made her urge Delia to leave. How long did they have? A few weeks? One week? A day? Something was coming for them, whether it was Delphine herself or one of her lackeys, Davena and Delia weren't long for this world.

What did she have to lose going after Beau? If he didn't want her, she would have lost nothing. If he did...then it was a small piece of pleasure in an otherwise hellish world. Only a fool would let something like that pass.

And her mother hadn't raised a fool.

Deciding to do it, and actually carrying through with her plan to kiss Beau was something altogether different. Impending death, however, put things into perspective.

She had been fool enough to believe she would

be able to lead an ordinary life, regardless of who her mother was. And her dear mother had allowed that belief to grow. The truth was that there was nothing normal or typical about them.

The last time she kissed a boy was the night her mother had died. Her boyfriend of more than a year had taken her on a date, except they hadn't gone to a restaurant. They had ended up on the banks of the Mississippi River where she had given him her virginity.

There had been one other instance during the past years where a man had pursued her. Davena had been so lonely that she had almost stayed with him. Where she kept her distance from men, Delia was the opposite. She would find one she was interested in, get him into bed, and then promptly ignore him the next day. It was her flippant attitude that had guys continuing to come after her.

Their mother's murder, and their close call with death had changed both sisters drastically. Neither was who they had been. The scars they bore were hidden within them. They were deeper, longer than the one on Davena's palm.

She fisted her scarred hand and rolled onto her side. Her gaze went to the door where she saw lights coming from the living room. She almost got up and tried to talk to Delia again, but she was tired of arguing. A good night's sleep would clear her mind.

Davena closed her eyes hoping for sleep. All she found were fantasies revolving around her and Beau.

~ ~ ~

Beau waited until he knew everyone had taken his or her beds and the house was quiet before he pulled his laptop from beneath his bed and quickly did a search for Davena again. He knew it wasn't a good sign that he couldn't get enough of her.

If he couldn't have Davena, the next best thing was a picture. He clicked on the images, scrolling through each one where she was wearing a brilliant smile. A few she was by herself. More often than not, she was with other girls, and some she was with a boy. He wore a letterman jacket and had short blond hair.

There wasn't a single picture of her newer than six years ago. It was like she dropped off the face of the earth. He couldn't help but wonder who had killed her mother. That's when he remembered that there was someone who might know more about the event. He reached for his cell phone and held it in his hand as he debated on whether to place the call or not.

He shoved aside his reservations and quickly dialed. With the phone to his ear, he listened to it ring once, twice.

On the third ring a deep voice answered over loud music, "It better be important for you to interrupt the plans I had tonight."

"She'll wait," Beau said with a smile.

The laugh was boisterous as the music faded with Court walking out of the pub he and his brothers owned called Gator Bait. "What can I do for you, cousin?"

Beau licked his lips. "Court, I need you to remember back six years ago."

"I'll try. What's this about?"

"A fire that burned a house and the women inside to ash. It was in Algiers."

There was a pregnant pause before Beau heard Court's loud sigh. "Ah, fuck. I wish I could forget that night. That was Babette Arcineaux's house. She and her daughters were killed."

Beau removed the computer from his lap and swung his legs over the side of the bed. "Was the fire an accident?"

"Not even close. Babette was a good woman. Unfortunately, she acquired a powerful enemy."

"Who?"

"Delphine."

Beau briefly closed his eyes. "The same Delphine that cursed Kane?"

"The very bitch," Court said, hatred dripping from his voice. "Why are you asking about something that happened six years ago? Does this involve Ava? Delphine swore to leave her alone."

"No," Beau hurried to explain. "Ava is doing fine so no need to worry her father. Delphine hasn't bothered her since y'all took care of things in New Orleans."

"What is family for? Besides, Delphine sent my brother after Ava."

"How is Kane?" Beau asked.

"He's...Kane. It isn't easy for any of us to deal with our curse. You'd think being a werewolf would have its advantages, but not so much."

"I'm sorry the LaRue's are dealing with that."

"It's not like you were the one to piss off a Voodoo priestess," Court joked. "Now, back to the Arcineaux's. Why do you want to know?"

Damn. Beau had hoped Court would let it drop. He should've known his cousin wouldn't let up so easily. "Are you sure the daughters died?"

"There was nothing left of the house, and neither Babette or her girls were seen again. Everyone assumed they died. You found the girls didn't you?"

"Maybe."

Court lowered his voice to a whisper. "Beau, if you have them, keep them safe. Delphine might still be after them."

"Why? What did the sisters do?"

"Isn't it enough that they have such a powerful enemy? Trust me, cousin, you don't want to get on Delphine's bad side. She never forgets or forgives. She holds a grudge forever, and revenge is second nature. All the Chiassons are already on her radar for interfering last time."

Beau wiped a hand down his face. "Yeah. After what she did to Kane, Ava, and Jack, I'm beginning to see that."

"Do we need to come down there?"

"No," he said firmly. "We've got something weird going on, and we think we've pinpointed a young family that could either be responsible or on the receiving end."

Court chuckled dryly. "Ah, but the Arcineaux

girls caught your attention. How did you piece it together? What name are they using?"

"Their own. They've been here for a little over a year."

"And you thought they could be in danger? No doubt they are. They have been since the night of their mother's death. As long as Delphine doesn't know they're alive, they'll be fine. I'd have thought they would be long gone from Louisiana though."

Beau did, as well. What kept them in the state and so close to someone as dangerous as Delphine? "Look, if you don't hear from any of us over the next few days, one of you might want to come check on things."

"Sounds like you've got something big in town. What is it?"

"I don't know." Beau rested his head in his hand. "Olivia's grandmother was here this morning after being woken by something."

"She's the one who practices Hoodoo, right?"

Beau nodded, and then said, "Yep. She got into it years ago when she had her own child. The thing is, Court, I woke up with a bad feeling, as well. And I smelled...smoke."

"Smoke?"

"That's not all. I just had a really bad feeling that grew as the day went on, but Maria had more information to impart. She said whatever is coming isn't here for us, but that we'll try to stop it and it'll turn its attention to us. She said that it would come for us, and that someone was going to be hurt."

"Shit. Maybe we should make another trip to

Lyons Point."

"I wouldn't mind the help, but y'all have your own problems. Just in case, if I haven't called to update you, check in on us."

"Will do. Tell me, are the sisters as pretty as they used to be?" Court asked.

Beau could hear the smile in his voice. "I suppose."

"You really need to work on your lying, cuz. Delia was pretty, but I always suspected it would be Davena who ended up being the beauty of the two. So, which one is the looker?"

"Davena." Beau hadn't had to think twice about it.

"I knew it."

Beau sat up and cleared his throat. "Thanks for the information."

"Anytime. Watch yourself, Beau."

"Same to you, Court."

He disconnected the call and set aside his phone. Beau leaned back against the headboard and settled his laptop back in place as he typed in Babette Arcineaux in the search engine.

CHAPTER NINE

Davena woke feeling rested and ready for a Saturday off. She didn't wake Delia as she tiptoed into the bathroom. She took her time in the shower, letting the hot water beat on her tense shoulder muscles. What she wouldn't do for a massage. It seemed like the most self-indulgent thing she could do for herself. It was also too pricey for her to even consider.

By the time Davena dried off and combed her hair, she was determined to put their argument behind them. She belted her robe and stepped out of the bathroom.

"Good morning," she called cheerfully as she went to turn on the coffee pot.

The next thing she was going to splurge on was a coffee pot with a programmable timer so the coffee would be waiting for them when they woke. As soon as the coffee began to brew, she drew in a deep breath and turned to the couch. It was empty, but that was nothing odd. Delia had always been an earlier riser.

Davena didn't think anything of it, thinking Delia went down the street to pet the horses. Davena decided to make some breakfast as she waited. That's when she determined it was time both she and her sister did something fun for themselves. And today was just the day.

She finished the eggs, and gave a shout to Delia that breakfast was ready in case she was outside. Davena tucked her wet hair behind her ear and hurried to the metal shelves against the wall. She grabbed an old leather bound book they had found at a flea market.

The pages had been half burned from a fire, and ruined from the water, but it was perfect for them. She had hollowed out the center to put their money in since they were never in one place long enough for a bank. Davena flipped open the cover and stared in disbelief. Every cent of their money was gone. Only a folded piece of paper remained.

Her hands shook as she pulled out the note. Discarding the book, Davena opened the note. She immediately recognized Delia's looping, whimsical handwriting. The note was simple. It read:

DAVENA —

IT'S FOR THE BEST. LET ME GO.

D.

The note fell from her numb fingers as her ears began to ring. It was all a dream. It had to be. She and Delia made a pact never to leave the other. Ever.

"No," she mumbled her eyes jerking to the

window.

In her haste to get to the window, Davena tripped over her feet that felt as if encased in concrete. She fell against the blinds awkwardly.

"Dammit!" she yelled while trying to open the blinds so she could see out.

Her heart was thudding in her chest when she finally got them open and saw the empty space in front of the house where their car was always parked.

Not only had Delia left with all their money, but she had taken the car as well. What was Davena supposed to do? She had nothing with which to pay the rent on Monday or for food. How was she going to go into work without a vehicle?

Her knees buckled and she fell to the ground, resting the side of her face against the wall. With no idea of where Delia could have gone, Davena didn't know where to begin looking. The questions rushing through her mind were so many and so loud, that she let herself zone out.

She didn't know how long the buzzing went on until she finally noticed it. Davena blinked, looking to the kitchen table where the pager the veterinarian gave them for emergency calls bounced around as it continued to vibrate.

Davena suddenly had a purpose. She climbed to her feet and walked to the table. 911 flashed on the screen when she answered it, which meant an animal had been brought in for an emergency. With nothing else to do, Davena rushed into the bedroom and threw on some clothes. She ran back into the kitchen, turned off the coffee pot, quickly made a sandwich out of the eggs she had cooked, and grabbed the house keys on her way out.

She ate as she walked into town. It was only a few miles, but what would take them only a couple of minutes by car, would take her much longer on foot. Running wasn't an option since she was eating, and she had to eat since she had no idea when she would be able to replenish the food. She knew what it was like to miss day's worth of meals, and she wasn't going to turn away food just because she wasn't hungry.

Incredulity over what Delia had done turned to fury, and then resentment.

She was about a mile from the house when a car slowed beside her and the window rolled down. Davena glanced over and saw it was the sheriff's department.

"Hello, ma'am," said the man with a tip of his hat as the car drove alongside her.

Davena stopped and forced a smiled as she faced him. "Good morning, sheriff."

"I'm just a deputy with the sheriff's department, ma'am. My name is Marshall Ducet. I'm new to the area, so I mean no disrespect when I ask if you need anything?"

She looked into his gray eyes. His black hair was short and held a wave to it. He had an easy, charming smile that she bet normally put people at ease. Young and handsome, Davena knew if he weren't already taken, he would be soon.

"Deputy, would it be too much trouble to ask

for a ride? My sister has taken the car, and Dr. Hebert has an emergency."

"The vet?" Marshall asked with a small frown. "Of course. Get in."

Davena started to grab the handle of the back passenger door when he laughed. She looked up, and he motioned her to come around to the front. She gladly rushed to the front passenger seat and got into the car.

After she buckled her seatbelt, she looked over at him to find him staring at her. "Oh. My apologies. It's been a...difficult morning. I'm Davena."

"What an unusual name. Do you have a last name to go with that?" he asked as he pressed on the accelerator.

She had given her name so many times over the last few years, but now she found herself hesitating. Davena decided to take another approach. If he thought her nervous, she knew he would continue to press her. "Must you know details of everyone who sits up here with you?" she asked with a grin.

He smiled and glanced at her. "I'm just curious. I come from a big city, so this is a change for me. I want to get to know everyone."

"You will soon enough."

"Are you a veterinarian yourself?"

It was Davena's turn to laugh. "No, though I do love animals. I help out in the office."

Thankfully, they pulled up to the clinic then. There were only two vehicles there. A tan heavy-duty truck that belonged to Dr. Hebert, and an older dark green Suburban.

"I appreciate the ride," Davena said and opened the door.

"My pleasure. Good luck in there," Marshall said with a nod.

Davena closed the door behind her and briefly watched him drive away before she ran into the clinic.

~ ~ ~

Beau smelled the smoke again. It was heavier, clinging to him. He couldn't take a breath, couldn't see. The smoke wrapped around him as if alive. He swatted at it, but he couldn't get free. It wound up his legs to his waist, clinging to him until he couldn't move. He tilted back his head in an effort to keep it out of his face, but there was no escaping it.

He was held immobile. Through the smoke, he could see a female dressed in white. No matter how hard he looked, he couldn't make out her face. Then the smoke took him to the ground and seeped into his mouth and nose and into his lungs. It was killing him, choking him.

Beau's eyes snapped open as he jerked upright in bed. Once more, he was drenched with sweat. He sucked in huge mouthfuls of air and hastily glanced around to make sure there was no smoke.

His door suddenly burst open as all three brothers bounded into his room. Lincoln was the first in, his boxers barely pulled over his hips while

Vincent's hair stuck up at odd angles as he began to search the room.

Beau watched them both with a mixture of annoyance and amusement. Christian was the only one who seemed to have things together. He leaned, fully dressed, against the doorway and cocked a brow.

"What the hell is going on?" Beau finally asked.

Vincent stood up from looking under the bed and raked his hair back. "What's wrong? You're the one who shouted."

"Yep," Lincoln said as he checked the connecting bathroom.

Beau remembered the dream clear as day, but he hadn't shouted. He had wanted to, but had been unable to do it.

"What happened?" Christian asked.

With all three of them staring at him, Beau knew he wouldn't get out of it unless he told them the truth. "It was a dream."

"A dream?" Vin repeated, skepticism thickening his voice.

Beau sighed and tossed off the damp sheet. He shoved Vincent out of the way and hastily stripped the sheets from the bed. That would make two days in a row with clean sheets. "Yes, a dream," he answered crossly.

Lincoln grabbed one of the pillows and pulled it out of its case. "What was the dream?"

Beau paused and closed his eyes as he recalled it with perfect clarity. "Smoke. It came for me like it was alive." He opened his eyes and looked at each of his brothers before he said, "It came to kill me."

"This could be what Maria meant," Christian said.

Vincent sank onto the mattress and shook his head. "What about that feeling you had yesterday, Beau? Do you still have it?"

He wanted to lie to Vin and tell him that it was gone, but that would put everyone in danger. "It's worse."

"Well, hell," Christian said. "What now?"

Lincoln ruffled Christian's hair. "We do what we do."

"Everyone meet downstairs in ten minutes. We need to find out more about the Dumas family."

Beau waited until everyone left his room before dropped his head. It wasn't just the smoke. Whoever had been in his dream was who controlled the smoke. She was the one meant to do harm, she was the one they needed to find.

If only he could've seen her face. The only thing discernible had been the fact she was female and dressed in all white. He couldn't tell his brothers that. It wasn't enough to go on.

~ ~ ~

Davena put her hands on the small of her back and stretched. A car had hit the German shepherd, but luckily its owner had been close and able to bring the dog in for surgery.

With Delia nowhere around, Davena had to stay with the dog until Sunday when Dr. Hebert came in to relieve her. She checked on the dog again before going to the kennels and taking one dog at a time outside.

She walked outside, surprised to find that night had already fallen. It had been well after noon before the surgery had been completed, and a few hours after that before either her or the doctor had been able to take a few moments and get something to eat.

The Pomeranian she was walking kept barking at something across the street. Davena peered into the darkness, but she couldn't see into the shadows.

"Just pee already," she urged the dog.

The small strip of grass left the animals little room to do their business. The dog growled and began to turn in circles before barking again, this time incessantly. Davena had no choice but to pick the dog up and try to quiet it. As she held it close, she could feel the animal shaking uncontrollably.

She looked from the dog to the shadows where he was still staring. Fear ripped through her. She clutched the dog, ready to bolt when something ran out of the shadows and beneath the next streetlight.

"A raccoon. It was only a raccoon," she said with a laugh.

The fear should've dissipated, but it didn't. It grew.

Davena turned and quickened her pace even as she walked back into the building. Not that it could keep her safe. Nothing would be able to keep her safe now.

CHAPTER TEN

"There's not a goddamn thing out here," Christian said, not bothering to whisper.

Vincent shot him a withering look. "They're the most likely ones. We agreed."

"That's a crock of shit. We three voted, Beau just nodded. He doesn't believe this Dumas family is our target."

Beau wanted to slam his fist into Christian's nose. "That's not true. I agreed that this family could be the target. Ava's connections found a lot of good evidence that pointed to them."

"Tell the truth, Beau," Linc said. "If it were up to you, would we be staking out the Dumas family tonight?"

Beau looked at the ground and blew out a breath. "No."

"Son of a bitch," Vincent mumbled as he turned his head away.

"I'm not going against you, Vin," Beau said hastily. "I don't know if I think it's Davena

Arcineaux because it is, or because..."

Shit. He couldn't even say the words aloud.

"He finds her interesting," Lincoln supplied for him.

Vincent met his gaze and nodded in understanding. "All right. You and Christian go into town and check on the Arcineaux sisters. Lincoln and I'll stay here."

Christian slapped Beau on the back and started across the field toward his truck. Beau looked at Vincent and Lincoln, unable to explain his need to get to Davena. He started to thank them, when a feeling of such hatred and evil rushed through him that it brought him to his knees. It clutched at his stomach, knotting it until he knew without a doubt that it wasn't the Dumas family they should be watching.

Beau looked up as his brothers grabbed him. "Davena," he said through clenched teeth.

"Christian!" Vincent bellowed.

Beau saw Christian run full tilt across the field to the truck while Vincent and Lincoln were on either side of him helping him walk.

"What is it?" Vincent asked.

Beau knew every moment they wasted was a second Davena and her sister were closer to death. "That feeling is back."

"It's not the Dumas family. I can hear the kids laughing all the way out here," Lincoln stated.

Christian's truck roared to life and came barreling toward them only to slide to a stop next to them. Beau was shoved in the front seat, and

Vincent and Lincoln got into the back.

"Hurry," Vincent said and grabbed the back of Christian's seat.

Christian floored the accelerator, bouncing them over the land until they rejoined the road. He sped down the road going over a hundred. "We've got company," Christian said.

Beau turned around and saw the flashing red and blue lights of the police. "Get me as close as you can."

"We don't even know where she lives," Lincoln said.

That was a mistake on Beau's part. He'd known she could be the target, but he'd been so intent on keeping his distance that he had failed to get the details. "I'll find her."

"I'm coming with you," Vincent said.

On the outskirts of town, Christian jerked the wheel and sent the truck into a spin. Beau opened the door and rolled out, landing hard on his shoulder on the concrete.

"Fuck," he muttered and jumped to his feet, his double-barrel sawed off shotgun in hand.

Vincent ran past him. "Hurry!"

Beau gritted through the pain in his stomach and his shoulder, and followed him into the shadows just as the sheriff's car pulled up behind Christian. There wasn't time to watch and see if his brothers could talk themselves out of going to jail.

"Which way?" Vin asked.

Beau looked first one way and then the other. "I don't have any idea."

"Start with what you do know."

"She works at the animal clinic." Beau fisted his hand in frustration.

Vincent grabbed him to keep him still. "Your feeling told you it was Davena and her sister, right?"

"Yes," Beau said hesitantly.

"Then trust that feeling to lead you to her now. For some reason the two of you are linked."

"Or it's just that we're both going to die by the same hand." Beau grimaced and turned away when he saw the look on Vincent's face.

Vincent unsheathed his machete. "You're not going to die. No one is going to die tonight."

"Then explain how I know these things?" Beau asked as he looked at Vin.

"I can't." His voice was calmer, composed. Vincent was once more in control of his emotions. "Find her, Beau."

Beau knew it was pointless. The knot in his stomach grew more and more painful, a warning that time was running out. He thought of her sexy voice and her amazing smile. What an idiot he was not to have touched her hair when he'd had the chance.

"It's no use," Beau said.

Vincent parted his lips to talk when a scream rent the air. Both turned in the direction of the sound and took off running. Beau prayed it wasn't Davena, and that they weren't too late.

They rounded the corner and saw a woman with her hand at her throat. "She just disappeared," she told the man beside. "Right in front of me!"

Beau exchanged a look with Vin and hid his shotgun against his other leg as they walked past. Only three blocks up was the animal clinic.

"Looks like we're on the right track," Vincent said.

"Looks that way."

"We'll get there in time."

Beau was beginning to doubt it.

~ ~ ~

Davena looked at the whining yellow lab. He pawed at the kennel door, his big gold eyes silently beseeching her. The last thing she wanted to do was go outside. It was silly to think that walls could keep her alive, but it was a lot like thinking if she kept her eyes closed, the monsters in her closet would never get her.

She even managed to remember a few of her mother's spells, not that it did her any good. She hadn't practiced in years, and without the practice, the spells wouldn't work. Death was death, no matter how it happened or when. She could remain in the clinic and take the chance that the animals were killed along with her, or she could go outside and face it.

Davena rested her forehead on the kennel. "I was going to get my hair done today," she told the lab. "I was also going to go to the Chiassons and find Beau. I'm not sure exactly what I was going to do once I was there, but I was going to do it today."

The dog cocked his head at her and whined again.

"All right," she said and grabbed a leash from the hook. She opened the kennel door and snapped the leash to his collar.

Davena gave him a good rub before she walked him to the door. On the way out, she checked on the shepherd to make sure he was still all right. With her hand on the knob of the back door, Davena hesitated a moment, and then cautiously opened it. Nothing jumped out at her. She barely had time to let her shoulders sag before the lab pushed his head through the opening and raced outside.

She caught the edge of the door with her fingertip and managed to swing it closed as she followed the dog. He went to the grass and lifted his leg against the lone tree. Her gaze scanned the area around her. The darkness concealed too much. It made her jumpy and edgy.

The lab finished and lifted his ears as he looked behind him. Davena turned, her blood turning to ice as she expected to see Delphine appear in front of her. She bit back a scream when she saw the all white clothes come out of the darkness. The dog jerked the leash out of her grasp as he raced to the figure.

Davena stood in shock as the dog sat in front of the person, tail wagging. She frowned and looked closer. That's when she realized it wasn't Delphine, it was her sister.

"Delia," she said, unsure of whether to be angry or relieved.

"It's me," her sister said and walked to her.

Davena started to speak, then stopped since she didn't know what to ask first.

"I had to," Delia said.

Davena rolled her eyes. "Had to what?"

"I had to do this. I had to prepare, and in order to do that, I had to leave you last night. It's going to end tonight for good."

"I hate riddles, Delia. Just tell me."

Delia smiled in triumph, her gaze over Davena's shoulder. She pointed. "Look for yourself."

Davena didn't want to turn around because she was afraid she knew exactly who was there. She slowly turned, and caught sight of Delphine herself, still looking as young and beautiful as she had six years before.

"Everything is going to be all right," Delia said as she came to stand beside Davena. "Trust me."

"Trust you?" Davena asked bewilderment.

Delia's brown gaze met hers. "I can do what our mother couldn't. I'm going to kill Delphine."

Davena reached for her sister, only to be thrown backward. She hit the side of the clinic, her head banging against the brick. The lab was by her side licking her face and nudging her with his cold, wet nose.

She opened her eyes, but everything was blurry. Unable to focus on anything, she patted the dog until she found his collar, and then the leash. With the building to steady her, she got to her feet and managed to find the back door. "Get inside," she told the lab, closing it behind him.

Davena turned around so fast that everything began to spin. She reached out for the building to steady her, but only grasped air. She could feel herself titling, falling.

Suddenly, strong hands steadied her, pulling her against a thickly muscled chest. "What hurts?" asked a rich, smooth voice she recognized instantly.

She looked up into Beau's intense blue gaze. "You're here. How is that possible?"

"Later. What hurts?" he asked again, his voice rough as if he were keeping something tightly leashed.

"My head. Delia threw me against the building."

His big hands gently smoothed back her hair. "My brother is going to get you out of here."

"No," she said with a shake of her head that she instantly regretted. "Delia's in trouble. I can't leave her."

"She's up against someone she can't handle," said another male voice as he stepped closer.

Davena recognized the eldest Chiasson brother, Vincent. "I can't leave her."

A muscle ticked in Beau's jaw as he simply stared. "If you stay, you could die."

"It's my sister. Would you leave one of your brothers?"

Beau gave a single shake of his head. "Never."

"Let's get Delia then," Vincent said.

Davena placed her hands on Beau's chest, feeling the heat of him through her palms. He took a breath, expanding his chest and causing his muscles to move beneath her hands. "It won't matter where you take us. Delphine knows we're here. Nothing will stop her now."

"So everyone keeps telling me," Beau said angrily.

Vincent's gaze narrowed on Beau. "Who precisely?"

Beau shrugged. "I might have called Court."

Vincent mumbled something in Cajun beneath his breath and peered around the edge of the building. "It's now or never."

"Go," Davena said and tried to push him away. "This isn't your fight."

Beau's blue eyes flashed dangerously. "How very wrong you are."

Davena wanted to stay with him, to see if he might lean down and kiss her. That would have been the easy thing to do. Instead, she stepped out of his arms. She could see clearly once again, and she would stand by her sister and face the bitch that murdered their mother.

She saw Beau's frown as he tried to figure what she was about. Davena took that second and rushed around the building in time to see Delia and Delphine face off. Delia was chanting, preparing a spell. She had only just begun, when Delphine lifted a hand in front of her and cupped the air. She then spread her fingers flat.

That same gnawing fear clawed at Davena that had been with her for days. She kept running toward Delia, even as Delia began to scream as she

bent over. Davena was steps away when her sister
burst into flames.

CHAPTER ELEVEN

Beau grabbed Davena before the flames could touch her skin and dragged her away.

"Nooooo!" she screamed, fighting him to get free.

He held Davena with one arm, her back against his chest while his other hand lifted the shotgun to aim it at Delphine. The priestess merely smiled at him, her face alight with exhilaration. The smoke that was drifting skyward suddenly shifted toward him.

Vincent knocked his gun down. "Don't be a fool."

Beau pulled his gaze from Delphine to focus on his brother. "I could end this."

"You'll get killed," Vin stated through clenched teeth.

Beau winced when one of Davena's feet connected with his shin. Delia's screams ceased. She fell to her knees, the flames so thick that he could no longer make out her features. The sound of quickly approaching footsteps had Beau shifting to aim his gun behind him. Vincent had his machete ready as he faced the oncoming threat.

They both lowered their weapons when they saw Christian and Lincoln. It was the man in a police uniform that came up behind them that caused worry.

Beau pulled his full attention back to Davena who was doing her damnedest to get free. A couple of times she nearly succeeded. "Stop," he whispered urgently in Davena's ear. "Her attention is focused on Delia right now, not you."

That just fueled Davena to fight him harder.

"What the fuck?" the sheriff's deputy asked as he rushed past them to Delia.

He tried to reach through the flames to Delia, but she fell to the side. "Get some water!"

One moment Beau was holding Davena, and the next he was flat on his back, the wind knocked out of him. He blinked and shook his head. When he looked up, he found his brothers and the deputy laid out as well. Only Davena remained on her feet.

He rose up on his elbow and watched as she walked to Delia. With words tumbling hurriedly from her lips, Davena put out the fire. Beau looked across the street to find Delphine's victorious smile gone, replaced with a look of utter incredulity.

"Did Davena just do that?" Christian whispered from beside him.

Beau nodded as he jumped to his feet and slowly started toward Davena. He still had his shotgun, not that it would do any good against

Delphine or even Davena. He halted behind Davena as she knelt beside Delia and took her sister's hand.

"Everything is going to be all right," Davena said.

Beau breathed through his mouth as the stench of burnt flesh reached him. He glanced at Delia to see there was no clothing, skin, or hair left.

"Let me go," Delia croaked.

Davena shook her head. "I'm going to make you better."

"You want to keep me in this kind of pain?" Delia asked brokenly.

"No, I'm —"

"You stopped the flames. Let them finish," Delia said hoarsely. "Please."

Beau's gaze latched onto Delphine. The Voodoo priestess wasn't done, but he didn't know if she would attack Davena that night or if she would wait.

"I love you, Delia," Davena said and rolled back onto the balls of her feet before standing.

As soon as she released Delia's hands, the flames returned. He stood beside Davena as she watched her sister burn, the life draining from her until nothing was left but a shell. The moment Delia's life ended, Delphine turned and vanished. But it wasn't the end. Things had just begun.

"What the hell just happened here?" demanded the deputy once he was on his feet.

"A shit storm," Christian answered.

Beau wanted to offer comfort to Davena, but

he didn't know if it would be welcome. She looked so forlorn standing there silently staring at her sister. There were no tears, just an absence of hope.

He finally gave in and wrapped an arm around her shoulders. When she didn't shrug him off, he stepped closer so their bodies touched. "I'm sorry."

"Beau," Vincent called.

He looked over his shoulder at his brothers to find the deputy staring at Davena. Beau nodded and turned Davena around to face them. She didn't fight him, didn't utter a word. He bent and glanced at her to see her gaze vacant.

"She's in shock," Lincoln said.

Christian snorted. "Hell, I think we all are."

"Someone tell me what just happened before I arrest you all," demanded the deputy.

Beau looked him over. He was well built, and wore his gun like a man who knew how to use it and wouldn't hesitate to do so. His black hair was kept short and combed back, and his wild gaze said he was on the edge of losing it all.

"Magic," Beau finally said. "You witnessed a powerful Voodoo priestess exact her revenge."

Lincoln cleared his throat. "Deputy Marshall Ducet, let me introduce my elder brother Vincent, and my youngest brother, Beau. The woman on his arm is —"

"Davena Arcineaux," Marshall interrupted in a calmer voice. "I gave her a ride to work this morning."

Beau tightened his hold on Davena. There was much about her he didn't know, but he wanted that to change.

"Voodoo," Marshall said and shook his head as he looked at the ground. "I left New Orleans to get away from that shit."

The brothers exchanged looks. It was Vincent who asked, "You were a cop in New Orleans?"

"For over seven years," Marshall said.

There was more to Marshall's story, but Beau was concerned with Davena right then. "We need to get off the streets and get Davena to the house."

"Agreed," Vincent said.

Christian looked at Marshall. "I wouldn't stay out here alone. She saw you with us."

The deputy shrugged. "I don't much care. Get out of here, all of you," he said as he looked around at them. "I'll get this cleaned up."

Beau didn't have to be told twice. He walked Davena to Christian's truck. He put her in the middle of the back seat and climbed in beside her. Lincoln sat on her other side, and as soon as Vincent shut his door, Christian drove them home.

The ride was made in silence, with each of his brothers casting furtive glances at Davena. To Beau's surprise, she reached over and took his hand. He wasn't sure she was even aware of it. She needed comfort from whoever would give it. And he was most willing to give it.

When they reached the house, Davena was still glassy-eyed from shock. Beau didn't ask, just gathered her in his arms and walked her inside the house. Ava and Olivia met them at the door, their questions coming all at once. Fortunately, Lincoln and Vincent were there to answer them.

Beau took Davena into the office and laid her on the couch. He took the throw off the back of the couch and draped it over her. Then he squatted beside her. He stopped himself from stroking a lock of her golden hair.

"You're safe here," he said, hoping she heard him.

He stood and sat in the chair next to the couch. The last thing he wanted was for her to come out of her shock and find herself alone in a strange house. Not to mention he wanted to be with her in any way that he could.

"How is she?" Olivia asked in a whisper from the doorway.

Beau shrugged helplessly. "Not good."

"I'll make some coffee. I have a feeling we're all going to need it."

Beau propped his elbow on the arm of the chair and dropped his head into his hand. He squeezed his eyes closed. Delphine had found the sisters. That was surprising enough, but not nearly so much as knowing that Delia tried to go up against the priestess with Hoodoo.

Then there was Davena. She was infinitely more powerful than her sister. She had shown that tonight by putting out Delphine's flames and knocking all of them on their asses. Why then didn't the sisters attack Delphine as one?

The minutes ticked by as the voices from the kitchen drifted into the room. His family was keeping their voices down, but he knew they were talking about the night's events. It wouldn't be long before they would want his take on things.

"I couldn't stop her," Davena suddenly said into the quiet.

Beau's eyes snapped open and he lifted his head to look at her. After a brief hesitation, he leaned forward so he could see her face. "Delphine can't be stopped."

"Delia. I couldn't stop Delia." Her voice was soft, grief filling every syllable.

Beau blew out a breath, unsure of what to say. "You're not responsible for her decisions."

"I should've known she would try something."

He was thinking of how to reply, when her hand reached out for his. Beau didn't hesitate to slide his fingers into hers.

"Tell me how you came to be there," she asked.

She might be looking at the empty fireplace, but he knew she could see his every move. Beau licked his lips. "The Chiassons have been protecting this parish for generations from the supernatural."

Her gaze snapped to his, a small frown forming between her eyes. "So you knew Delphine was here?"

"No," he hurried to say. "We knew something was here, but we didn't know what or who."

"Yet you were there tonight. It wasn't by accident."

Beau paused. He hadn't liked explaining what had been happening to him with his family. He certainly wasn't keen on sharing it with Davena.

"Tell her," Lincoln said from the doorway.

Davena looked from Beau to Lincoln and then slowly sat up, removing her hand from his. Then her gaze came back to Beau. "Tell me what?"

Beau fisted the hand that had held hers, hating how much he missed the contact, and slowly sat back. "I had a feeling it was you."

"It was far from a feeling," Lincoln said and walked into the room. "He's had dreams of smoke. Tonight, while we were watching someone else, he doubled over in pain, telling us we had to get to you."

Beau couldn't stand Davena's troubled eyes on him. He rose and walked to the desk on the other side of the room. How was it he had to put distance between him while needing to have her close?

"How is that possible?" Davena asked.

Lincoln said, "I thought you might tell us."

Beau kept his back to her, afraid to look at her again and not touch her. And if he got close enough to touch her, he wasn't sure if he could keep from pulling her close and kissing her. Here he was thinking of her lips and tasting her when she was dealing with the death of her sister and the arrival of Delphine. If she knew his thoughts, she would never let him near again.

"I don't know," she finally answered.

A sound from the doorway drew his gaze. Beau found the rest of his family standing there waiting. It was Olivia who walked into the room with a mug of coffee that she set on the coffee table.

"I thought you might need that," Olivia told

Davena

Beau turned just enough to see Davena. She eyed the coffee and then looked at Olivia. "I could use something much stronger, actually."

"We've got that, too," Christian said as he moved to the cabinet near the desk and poured a glass of bourbon. His eyes briefly met Beau's.

Unable to help himself, Beau turned around and let his gaze settle on Davena. Her blonde hair fell like gold around her shoulders. She kept her legs tucked against her and used the throw like a shield.

Her hands shook a little as she took the proffered liquor from Christian. She took two sips before she let out a wobbly breath and met his stare. "You know what happened in Algiers, don't you?"

Beau nodded. "You and Delia were safe all this time. Why draw Delphine out now?"

"I didn't. Delia did." Davena looked down at her hands. "I knew something bad was coming. I even knew it was Delphine, but Delia didn't want to leave."

Ava took the chair Beau had vacated and laid a comforting hand on Davena's arm. There was no need for words. The action said it all.

Beau walked to the desk and leaned against it. "Do you know what you did tonight?"

"Did?" Davena asked, her gaze jerking to him.

"You stopped Delphine's fire."

CHAPTER TWELVE

It wasn't possible. Davena wasn't powerful enough to even think about going up against someone like Delphine. She looked into Beau's fierce blue eyes and wished he were still beside her. His warmth and comfort were all that kept her from losing herself.

"You're mistaken." She took a large swallow of the bourbon and felt it burn down her throat and settle warmly in her stomach. "I don't have that kind of ability. My mother, perhaps."

"And Delia?" Vincent asked.

Just thinking about her sister brought an ache to her chest. She wanted to cry for all the years her sister had lost, but no tears would come. Davena grinned ruefully. "She thought she did, but she didn't. Our mother didn't want either of us involved in what she did."

"Which was what, exactly?" Christian asked.

When she heard Beau's growl directed at his brother for such a question, it eased some of the numbness gripping her. She knew it had been Beau who came to her and placed his arm around her, who walked her to the truck, and who carried her inside the house. He had stayed with her, silent and patient.

"My mother got into the Voodoo religion when she was thirteen," Davena said as she studied the gold liquid in her glass. "She had an affinity for the...other side of the religion. Soon, others were coming to her for spells and dolls. It wasn't until she met my father when she was eighteen that something changed. She never told us what, but she backed away from the religion."

Lincoln rubbed his hand over his jaw, his palm scratching along his whiskers. "I gather there were those upset by her move."

"I guess." Davena shrugged. "She didn't like to talk about it. It was part of her past we knew never to speak of while growing up. A year later, when she was nineteen, she married my father and got out of Voodoo altogether. Yet people still came to her for help. That's how she turned to Hoodoo. Some of her friends were being cursed because of their connection to her. She didn't think that was fair, so she found a way to counter it."

"Brave woman," Beau said.

Everyone else in the room was forgotten as she looked at him. How she wanted to run her hands through his hair and draw him close. She imagined he would kiss like he lived – softly at first, and then full throttle. "She was. She put her very life on the line every day. She saved a lot of people in the process."

"Did things change when you and Delia were born?" Ava asked.

Davena stiffened as she remembered it wasn't just her and Beau. "Not really. My father owned a restaurant in the French Quarter, and mother went on as she was, bringing in a little extra money in the process. That continued until I was four. I don't know why things changed that summer, but they did. It began when my father was killed in an alley outside his restaurant. He was found with his throat slit, and Voodoo markings painted in white all around him."

"It was a warning," Christian said.

"One my mother heeded in her own way. She stopped being so blatant about helping those who had been cursed, and took over the restaurant. Delia and I forgot all about the spells being practiced in our kitchen and became like every other little girl."

Davena took another long drink, coughing as it made her eyes water with the burn. She blinked away the moisture and tried not to stare at Beau. Still, he drew her gaze like a horse to water. She didn't know what it was, but she had to know him. It felt like...destiny. Fate even.

Abruptly, Beau walked to her and took the now empty glass as he sat on the coffee table. She was caught in his magnetic blue gaze. He asked, "Then what happened?"

"For thirteen years, nothing. We knew our mother would occasionally help someone by meeting them at the back of the restaurant, but she kept that very hush-hush. Delia had graduated a few months before, and I had just started my senior year. Mom began to act strangely, telling us to make sure no one was following us. I knew something was going to happen."

He set the glass beside him, never taking his eyes from her. "How?"

"A feeling. It began simply as a niggling that I promptly forgot. Every day it grew worse until it was knotted in my stomach. Mom thought someone had hexed me. She made me and Delia a mojo bag to carry around for protection."

"It wasn't a hex."

She shook her head. "Delphine is known all around New Orleans. I'd seen her multiple times, and knew she was someone not to be messed with. That night, before Mom was killed, I knew it was Delphine who would show up."

"Did you and Delia try to stop Delphine then?" Ava asked.

Davena couldn't stop the laugh that bubbled forth. She covered her mouth and briefly closed her eyes before she gave a quick shake of her head. "No. Our mother taught us a few things for safety, but she told us not to get involved with any of it. I didn't, but I didn't know Delia had been following her for years and memorizing spells."

Beau took her right hand and spread her fingers. His gaze dropped to her mouth before his eyes lowered to her palm. "You got this that night."

"Mom tried to counter Delphine, but Delphine

was too powerful."

The memories of that night mixed with recent ones, and she shivered at how similar her mother and sister acted as the fire consumed them. It was Beau's thumb slowly rubbing circles on her palm that slowed her breathing. She was transfixed, watching his thumb stroke over the burned portion of her palm to the normal skin. When she dared to look at him, she was struck by a blatant, deliberate desire.

Davena swallowed, her heart racing for an entirely new reason now.

"How did you get out?" Christian asked.

His words shattered the daze she was in, and she looked away, only to have her gaze skate right back to Beau. "The house began to burn with the unholy fire Delphine caused. Our mother knew something could attack at the house, so she dug a tunnel that led underground from her bedroom to the drainage ditch nearby. I grabbed the door that hid the tunnel, forgetting the metal handle would be hot."

"But you got out," Vincent said. "That in itself is a miracle."

"You should've gone to the authorities."

The new voice had every head turning to the doorway where Davena saw Deputy Ducet standing with his hat in his hands.

"You've overstepped, man," Christian said as he started toward Marshall.

Vincent interceded and stepped between the two. He put a hand to Christian's chest before he faced the deputy. "I agree with my brother. The polite thing to have done would've been to knock."

"I did," Marshall said and shifted his weight to his other foot. His eyes landed on Davena. "I was one of the officers who scoured your house for remains. We all thought you were dead."

She remained where she was because Beau still held her hand. His gaze urged her to stay as she was, to trust him. He had promised she was safe there, and for some reason she believed him.

"State your business, deputy," Beau said.

Marshall licked his lips. "Miss Arcineaux, your sister has been taken to the county morgue. I didn't think you wanted any more attention on this, so her death has been ruled an accident."

"How did you pull that off?" Lincoln asked.

Marshall turned his cowboy hat around in his hands. "The sheriff has been ready to retire for three years, and the other deputies are either so new they don't know their ass from a hole in the ground, or so old they don't give a shit anymore. With my time in New Orleans, they take my word for things. Not to mention, as soon as I mentioned the Chiasson name, they forgot all about it."

Olivia harrumphed. "I don't know whether to be grateful or angry that we have such men patrolling the streets."

"Sweetheart, why do you think we hunt?" Vin asked with a wink that made Olivia grin.

Ava stood and smiled at Marshall. "I'm sure you could use a cup of coffee, deputy. Let's give Davena a few minutes."

Davena smiled appreciatively at Ava as everyone filed out of the room. Everyone, that is, except for Beau. Now that they were alone, she had a hard time keeping eye contact.

"Do you want to be alone?" he asked.

"No," she answered quickly. Then she met his gaze and said in a steady voice, "No."

"You are safe here. This house is warded, blessed, and spelled. Nothing can come in."

"Our house was the same, and Delphine didn't have to come inside to kill my mother."

Beau sighed and looked down at her scar. He ran his thumb along the scar again. "We've had a recent dealing with Delphine. We'll figure this out."

"What you should do is throw me out and forget you ever knew me. If not, she'll come for you."

"Let her."

Davena's stomach fluttered as if a thousand butterflies had taken flight. Before her sat the man she had intended to come here and see that night. Nothing had gone as planned, and yet somehow, she still ended up in his arms. But she wanted more.

Her eyes lowered to his wide lips. She had watched her sister die, and knew that Delphine would be coming for her soon. No longer would fear hold her back. If she didn't take what was before her, she would die without ever knowing the feel of Beau's lips on hers.

Davena leaned forward and took her free hand to rest it on his cheek. His brilliant blue eyes darkened as desire flared. It was the boost to her courage that she needed. Her fingers trailed along his jawline to lips that were as soft as velvet.

"I was going to come here tonight," she confessed with a little smile. "I don't know what I would've said or how I would have gotten your interest."

"You've always had my interest."

The truth shone in his eyes. Davena slid her fingers into the hair at his temples and then down the strands that ended at his chin. "I don't know what tomorrow holds, and right now I don't care."

Before she could think twice about it, she leaned forward and gently placed her lips on his. She began to pull back, only to have him roughly haul her against his chest. Her arms wound around his neck for balance as she ended up fully in his lap. His gaze met hers for an instant before his lips took hers. He captured, he seized.

He claimed.

And Davena gloried in every wonderful moment of it.

His hands splayed on her back, holding her firmly against him while his head titled to the side. His kiss was electric. Then he changed everything by deepening the kiss, a moan rumbling from his chest as she eagerly opened for him.

Davena had never experienced anything so thrilling, so stirring. She felt alive for the first time in six years. The world and all her problems melted away. She let her hands roam over his thick shoulders, marveling at the strength she felt beneath her palms. His thin, black shirt only accentuated his finely honed body.

Desire, thick and needy, blossomed within her. It tightened low in her belly, as the kiss grew fiery and frantic. A wordless, urgent hunger had taken both of them, refusing to let go.

Her breath stopped when he caressed her back, his hands stopping at her side with his thumb grazing the bottom of her breast. He ended the kiss and looked at her with those incredible blue eyes of his.

Then he cupped her breast and ran his thumb over her nipple.

CHAPTER THIRTEEN

Beau was focused on the woman in his arms. It might have been Davena that kissed him, but there was no turning back for him now. He'd had a taste of her, and he had to have more. Her spring green eyes were dilated as she stared at him. Her lips were parted and wet from their kisses. Her breathing ragged, her pulse jumping wilding at the base of her throat.

The feel of her nipple beneath his palm through her shirt and bra about did him in. It was all he could do not to toss her on the couch and rip her clothes from her body before he thrust inside her.

He had felt desire before, but nothing came close to the all-consuming craving that burned within him for Davena. There was nothing that could pull him away from her, nothing that could make him release her.

Nothing that could ever wipe out the taste of her kiss.

Beau massaged her breast, his balls tightening

when a soft moan fell from her lips. It was wrong for a woman to be so beautiful and tempting. How was he expected to string together rational thoughts? He was only a man, after all.

He was so engrossed with Davena that he almost didn't hear the squeak in the wood floors as someone approached. Here he was, sitting with her across his lap stealing kisses and touches like he was still in high school.

There was no time for an explanation. Beau quickly set her back on the couch and jumped up to stand in front of the hearth. He kept his back to the door so no one would see his arousal.

"Marshall is leaving," Vincent said from the door.

When Davena didn't respond, Beau glanced at his brother over his shoulder. "You filled him in then?"

"On us?" Vin asked. "Of course. We've always kept the local law enforcement apprised of what we do, you know that."

Beau knew a lot of things, but he couldn't seem to make his brain function correctly. "Right."

"Is everything all right?" Vin asked suspiciously.

"It's fine," Beau and Davena said in unison.

Vincent snorted loudly. "Right. That was convincing."

Beau let out a sigh when Vincent walked away. He turned to Davena. Even now it was difficult to keep his distance.

"The animals," she suddenly said. Her face filled with distress. "I've got to stay with them. One dog was in surgery. I can't believe I forgot about them."

A problem. Beau was good at solving problems. Plus, it gave him something to focus on rather than Davena and the need clawing at him. "I'll take care of it."

He started for the door when she rose and walked with him into the foyer were Marshall stood with the rest of the family. The sheriff's deputy turned his attention to them.

"I left New Orleans because most of the cops turned a blind eye to Delphine," Marshall told Davena. "The other half was paid off as only someone like Delphine could do. The few of us who wanted to do honest work couldn't. Like with what happened to your mother."

Davena crossed her arms over her chest. "One man can't expect to change a city."

"I came here expecting it to be different." Marshall looked around and smiled ruefully. "I guess it is. I never knew there were those like the Chiassons around."

Christian smiled crookedly. "Do you remember any LaRue's in New Orleans?"

Marshall's lips flatted. "Yes. Why?"

"They're our cousins," Lincoln said. "And they do what we do."

"Then they need to do a better job of it," Marshall said. He put his hat on and nodded to the women. "Good night all."

Beau waited until the door closed behind the deputy before he said, "I'm heading out too."

There was a lengthy stretch of silence as every eye turned to him. Finally, it was Lincoln who asked, "Why?"

"I need to go to the animal clinic. Davena was supposed to stay there all night and watch over the animals. She's not leaving the house."

Vincent widened his stance and looked from Davena to Beau. "This is the safest place for Davena. I don't think it's a good idea for you to be out there either."

"Someone has to be there until the doc arrives at seven," Davena said. "I can't have those animals left alone. As I told Beau, it doesn't matter where I am or how safe it is. Delphine will come for me whenever she wants."

Christian threw his keys up in the air and caught them. "I'll go."

"Dammit, Christian," Vincent said angrily.

Beau held up a hand to quiet everyone. "He goes or I do, because if we don't, Davena will."

Davena nodded in agreement.

Without another word, Christian turned on his heel and walked out the back door. Beau wasn't sure if he should be relieved that he stayed behind, or concerned about how he was going to get through the rest of the night.

"There's food in the kitchen," Olivia said. "Beau made the best banana pudding I've ever had. There is still some chicken left, as well."

Ava scrunched up her nose. "Actually, Christian and Marshall finished off both."

"I can fix her whatever she wants," Beau said.

Davena cocked her head at him. "You cook?"

"He's the best around," Lincoln said.

Vincent nodded. "He does the lion's share of the cooking around here. He's got a gift."

"Is that so?" Davena said, a small smile playing at her lips. "Thank you for the offer, but I don't think I could eat."

Beau inhaled and looked at the stairs. "I'm sure you want to rest."

"I thought we'd put her in Riley's room," Ava said.

Olivia came to stand next to Davena. "We'll take her up now and show her around."

Beau watched the three of them ascend the stairs, his gaze locked on Davena's hips as they swayed side to side.

"You are so screwed," Vincent said as he came to stand on Beau's left.

Lincoln moved to Beau's right. "Actually, he won't be tonight."

Beau rolled his eyes as his brothers laughed at the joke. "Y'all are fucking hilarious."

~ ~ ~

Davena was ashamed. She knew she should be overcome with sadness after Delia's death, but all she could think about was Beau.

She walked next to Ava and Olivia as they pointed out each of the rooms upstairs in the old plantation house. She was the last to walk into the room kept for the lone female Chiasson. The white, iron bed was set against the far wall with a large floral print comforter in bright pink.

The room held several boxes stacked against one wall, but it was sparse other than a table next to the bed with a lamp and a picture frame. Davena walked to the table and sat on the bed as she lifted the frame.

She smiled at the picture that was about twenty years old judging by the young faces and the style of clothes. She looked at all five Chiasson children surrounding their parents, the smiles wide and infectious.

Davena easily picked out Beau despite all the siblings having the same dark hair and blue eyes. It wasn't a matter of narrowing it down. It was the way Beau smiled. It was warm and welcoming with a hint of waywardness.

It was a smile she had seen herself.

"They were a close family," Olivia said.

Ava sat beside Davena. "Olivia knew them from growing up here, but I only knew their reputation within the parish. They're still close, despite what happened to their parents."

"What happened?" Davena was intrigued. Besides, it would take her mind off of Beau and Delia.

Olivia sat on the opposite side of the bed and rested her arm on the tall footboard. "They were murdered on the same night by a woman who lusted after their father for herself."

"That's horrible," Davena said and shifted to see both women. "How long ago was that?"

"A week after that picture was taken," Ava replied softly.

Davena glanced back at the picture. "Worlds can crumble in an instant, can't they?"

"Both mine and Ava's did. Then our men found us," Olivia said with a bright grin.

Ava winked at Davena. "Just as Beau found you."

Beau. She licked her lips, still feeling his on hers. His kisses had literally curled her toes. She hadn't been able to remember her name, but the one thing she knew with certainty was that she wanted to kiss him forever.

"Once Delphine decides to come for you, nothing will change her mind," Davena said.

Ava shrugged one shoulder. "She was after me, but the LaRues managed to change her mind."

Davena studied Ava closely, trying to determine how much to tell her. "I've never heard of her giving up on someone unless there was a trade made."

"Trade?" Olivia repeated frowning.

"A trade that was worth it to Delphine," Davena explained. "If she was out to kill someone, then someone would have to know the whereabouts of an individual she sought, or offer something else of similar value."

The two women exchanged a look as Ava's face grew pale. "They told me Delphine released me after they captured her."

"Captured Delphine? No one captures her unless she wants to be caught." Davena wasn't trying to start trouble, but everyone needed to understand the danger Delphine posed.

Olivia rubbed her hand up and down Ava's arm. "We don't know who lied, so don't get angry yet. It could be that Delphine was playing everyone."

"She does that well enough," Davena said.

Ava took in a shaky breath. "So you've had several dealings with her?"

"A few," Davena replied. "She is a mainstay in the French Quarter. She's famous and greatly feared. Those who practice the Voodoo religion worship her for her great powers. She always knows a person's weakness. That's how she gets so many to do as she wants."

"So you've never met her personally?" Olivia asked.

Davena replaced the frame and rose to look out the window. A scene of tranquil beauty met her gaze as she looked out over the moon-drenched bayou. "There were a couple of instances where I spoke with her. Not even my mother knew. Once, I was twelve. I walked out of school waiting on Delia and there Delphine was."

"What did she want?" Ava asked.

Davena fingered the lace curtains. "I don't know. She asked me silly questions like how I did in school and if I was happy. She freaked me out so much that I walked away while she continued to ask questions."

"And the next time?" Olivia asked.

She faced the bed, her hands resting on the

windowsill. "I was sixteen. I'd been out late with friends and walking home. One moment my friends were talking, and the next they were on the ground unconscious. This time she asked if I was practicing my magic."

Ava blinked in shock. "Magic? I mean, I know what the guys said they saw you do tonight, but does that mean you know magic?"

"No," Davena said quickly. "I don't know how I did what I did tonight. I wanted to go to Delia, and I wanted the fire to stop. Somehow, both happened."

Olivia fluffed the pillows on the bed. "She took an interest in you. Did she do the same to Delia?"

"Not that I knew of, and Delia would've said something. She so desperately wanted to follow in our mother's footsteps," Davena said, remembering it all as if it just happened yesterday.

"What will you do now?"

Davena looked around the room. "As beautiful as this plantation is, I can't stay here."

CHAPTER FOURTEEN

Beau stared at the stove for a long time. Whenever he was troubled, he had always found solace in cooking. That night was the exception.

His body had yet to cool from his kisses with Davena, and knowing she would be sleeping down the hall from him wasn't making things any easier. But it was the knowledge that they hadn't seen the last of Delphine that turned the knot in his stomach tighter.

A glance at the clock showed he had been standing in the kitchen for almost two hours. Everyone else had long since found their beds. Beau didn't want to walk up the stairs because it would put him too close to Davena.

She should have time to herself after losing her sister, not be pawed at by the likes of him. Beau couldn't believe he had groped her so. She had wanted a kiss, and he had taken things much further. If she were interested in him before, she certainly wouldn't be anymore. Perhaps it was for the best. Allowing anyone close was setting himself up for hurt later down the road.

He fisted his hand, the weight of her breast still fresh in his memory. She wasn't just beautiful, she was a fighter, a woman who never gave up. She was tenacious, steadfast, faithful, and trustworthy.

Davena had survived the worst kinds of travesty – twice – and still resolutely faced the world with her shoulders back and chin held high. He didn't know how she did it. His parents' deaths had nearly destroyed him and the family. Looking back, it was his siblings that kept him going.

That he and Davena had in common, at least.

A sound coming from the study had Beau turning around and silently walking out of the kitchen. He sidestepped the creaking floorboard and stopped beside the open doorway of the office. A lamp on the far side of the room chased away the dark, and the desk light had been turned on granting him enough light to see who was in the study. He spotted Davena near the sideboard that held all the liquor. She took a long drink of bourbon before setting the glass down.

Her head turned to the side, just now noticing that she was no longer alone. "I thought I was the only one up."

"I never went up to bed." Beau stepped into the room and leaned back against the doorjamb. "Can't sleep either?"

Her glorious mane of golden hair shifted along her back as she shook her head. "Every time I close my eyes I see Delia in flames or lying burnt on the ground. I want to cry, but I can't."

"It'll come."

She chuckled dryly. "Will it? I can't feel anything. I'm numb, and I fear I'll remain that way until Delphine finally comes for me." Davena turned slowly to the side and looked at him. "It won't be here, though. I don't want her evil touching this place. You have a good thing here with your family."

"This land and this house were built and protected to help people like you."

"Like my mother helped people?" She twisted her lips in a rueful smile. "Take it from me, Beau. You don't want any part of that."

He glanced around the room thinking back to his early years when he had played in there just to be near his father while he poured over the journal. "Do we really have a choice? Ever since the first Chiasson came to this parish we've been protecting the people from the supernatural, whether it's ghosts, demons, creatures, or magic. We've saved a lot of people."

"And lost family."

"Yes," he answered after a short pause. "It's the price we pay for the hunting that we do."

She turned the glass in her hand, gazing down at it. "Despite the tragedies, Vincent and Lincoln have found women to call their own. What about the rest of you?"

"Christian won't. He refuses. Riley? She's being kept away from this, so I'm sure she will find someone, as well."

Davena's gaze lifted to his. "And you?"

A day ago he'd have said he agreed with Christian, but now, he was no longer sure of anything. "I don't know."

"Because you haven't found anyone?"

"Because I don't want to give my heart to someone only to have them taken away."

She looked away, taking a quick drink and then licking her lips. "I see."

"No, you don't."

Her gaze skated back to his. "Tell me then."

Beau hesitated, unsure of what he was doing. "I thought I would be all right alone. I was prepared for it. I just wasn't prepared for you. I don't want you close, but it's where I need you."

For long moments, their gazes held. Beau anxiously waited for her to respond, to say something, anything after he put out a statement like that. Finally, she set down her glass and pushed away from the sideboard. She closed the distance between them, stopping a few paces away from him.

"I have a hole inside me," she said softly. "It's growing by the minute. I haven't felt anything since I saw the flames take Delia, except when I was in your arms. I don't want to be alone tonight. I don't want to think of what happened or what is coming. I want...you."

Beau reached out, cupped her cheek and slid his hand into her hair, the silky strands gliding through his fingers. He understood all too well what she was going through – and what she wanted.

He stepped closer, pulling her against him as he did. Her spring green eyes drew him in until he was engulfed in all that was Davena. Her lips parted, drawing his gaze. His head dipped and he took her mouth. He tried to be gentle, to go slow, but at the first touch of their lips, her arms snaked around his neck. With her body molded to his, the passion erupted like a firestorm.

Beau held her tightly against him. He kissed her fiercely, brutally. All the while, her hands clawed at his shirt, ripping it in her efforts to take it off.

He pulled back long enough to remove the garment. With chests heaving, he paused before he kissed her again and felt something break apart inside him when she smiled. His hands rested on her hips and stroked upward until he reached the hem of her shirt. He slipped his fingers beneath it to touch her stomach.

Beau couldn't wait to strip her slowly of clothes, but that fantasy shattered when she jerked off her shirt and shimmied out of her jeans. In a matter of seconds, she stood before him in nothing but her yellow panties and bra.

Her smile mixed with the blatant desire shining in her eyes, and Beau forgot all about his fantasy. He hastily removed his jeans and yanked her to him. Then, with a twist of his fingers, he released her bra. The straps sagged on her shoulders, causing her grin to widen. She carelessly discarded it over her shoulder.

With nothing separating them other than the silk of her panties, Beau slowly ran his hand up her back. It brought her against him, pressing her breasts to his chest.

The passion was explosive, the desire sizzling. Each kiss brought them higher, closer. Her skin was satin, her touch scorching.

He turned her against the wall and kissed down her neck to her chest. Beau stopped long enough to suckle on each nipple, flicking his tongue over the tiny buds until she was gasping and her hips rocked against him.

Only then did he continue his kisses down her stomach and over her hips, tugging her panties down as he did, until he reached the golden curls nestled between her legs. He lifted one of her legs and draped it over his shoulder. Then he licked her. She cried out, her fingers tightening in his hair. But he didn't stop. He licked, he laved.

The taste of her essence was everything he'd known it would be and more. It wasn't enough to have her on his tongue, he wanted to feel her as well. With his tongue intent on her clitoris, he slid a finger inside her.

Davena clung to him as her body shivered with his every touch. Heat filled her until her veins ran with it. Her hips rocked in time with his tongue teasing her.

Her eyes closed as the pleasure became too much. She could feel her body rising to the climax, knew it was there waiting. He spread her legs wider, opening her more to his mouth so he could learn every inch of her.

Then his fingers began to explore her, working

her into a frenzy. She slammed her hands on the wall in an attempt to stay upright.

The bliss was intoxicating, the decadence exhilarating.

She was helpless to stop the unrelenting pleasure Beau heaped upon her. She might be powerless, but she'd never felt so safe. It gave her the freedom to open herself to him in ways she never imagined she could – or even knew she wanted to.

The orgasm, when it hit, took her breath. She opened her mouth on a silent scream as she was swept along a tide of unbelievable, incredible ecstasy.

Her knee buckled, but Beau caught her, shifting her until her legs wrapped around his waist. She opened her eyes to see him looking between them. Davena was enraptured as she watched the tip of his engorged cock slip through the folds of her sex and then inside her body.

She bit her lip as he filled her, stretching her. Her nails sank into his shoulders, even as she moaned in pleasure. Sweat glistened over their bodies, allowing them to slide easily against the other.

Beau's strong hands held her steadily as he suddenly turned away from the wall and walked to the couch. Each movement from him made his cock shift inside her, causing her to gasp and groan at the feel of it.

He sat down so that she straddled his hips and kissed her slowly, languidly. They used that time to learn each other. Davena hadn't gotten nearly enough time to look over his amazing body. His muscles were toned and powerful, the sinew molded tightly.

She ran her hands along his chest and over his washboard stomach before caressing the bulging muscles of his arms and shoulders. He abruptly ended the kiss and shifted them so that she was on her back on the couch, with him still inside her. His hands held her arms above her head as his gaze caught and held hers.

Then he began to move his hips. Long, slow strokes that heated her blood soon turned into hard, short thrusts that took her higher and higher.

She locked her ankles around his waist. His eyes darkened and his rhythm quickened. He filled her again and again, harder, deeper.

Davena turned her head into the couch when the scream welled up as her second climax claimed her. Her body pulsated with unending pleasure.

"Davena," Beau whispered.

She looked up to find his face contorted as he jerked, his own orgasm descending.

When he collapsed on her, Davena pulled her hands from his grasp and wound her arms around him, holding him. She knew they had been careless and didn't use protection. It wasn't as if it mattered. She would be dead soon anyway.

He settled against her with his head on her chest. Davena caressed his back with one hand, and leisurely, softly scraped her fingernails against his scalp as she played with his long, dark locks.

She tried to find regret, since it was something she always did, but there wasn't anything she regretted since arriving at the Chiasson plantation. Beau might be strong as an ox with enough bravery and courage to rival a superhero, but he was just as broken and battered as she was.

They were two of a kind.

It was too bad there wouldn't be a future for them.

~ ~ ~

The moonlight didn't penetrate the thick branches of the live oak. An owl hooted from one of the many branches, some so heavy they touched the ground. Delphine paid the animal no attention. Her focus was on the plantation where Davena had been brought.

The Chiassons. She had expected that they would interfere, just as their meddling cousins the LaRues often did. Yet there was something different about one of the Chiassons. It was the way he had looked at Davena, as if he would readily take on the world for her.

Delphine smiled slowly. She would see just how far he would go for Davena.

CHAPTER FIFTEEN

Beau opened his eyes to find Davena lying on her side facing him, her eyes open. Sometime in the night they had moved to the floor to sleep. His hand rested on her waist while hers lay near his face. She grinned, her eyes crinkling slightly at the corners.

"Did you sleep at all?" he asked.

She shrugged and held the blanket over her breasts. "No. I did try. It wasn't easy with you snoring."

"I would never," he teased, grateful that she didn't seem as weighted down that morning.

The smiles died as they gazed into each other's eyes, desire flaring to life once more. Beau pulled her closer and kissed her softly.

She scraped her fingers along his jaw over his whiskers. "What happens now?"

"Breakfast," he said. "I'll make you anything you want."

"A man who cooks. I could easily get spoiled."

He wanted more than anything to keep her beside him. What an idiot he had been to think he could remain alone. Davena was his. He knew it, but couldn't begin to explain how. "Then let me spoil you."

Davena looked away and sat up, keeping the blanket against her bare breasts. "Is that a good idea? For either of us?"

Beau rolled over and got to his feet. He knew she was pulling away from him, and even though he had fought against her pull, now that he had learned what it felt to have her in his arms, he wasn't ready to let her go without a fight.

He tugged on his jeans and tossed her a smile. "I'll get breakfast started if you want to grab a shower."

"Beau," she said and lifted her gaze to him. "It's a matter of hours before Delphine comes for me."

"We'll pay for Delia's funeral." If he ignored her, she might forget about wanting to put distance between them. Getting her to remain at the house might give him time to make her realize he could keep her safe.

She ran her hands through her long hair and sighed. "Fine. We'll do this your way."

Beau kept his smile in place until he was in the kitchen. Once there, he closed his eyes and knew he was in the biggest fight of his life — two-fold. Not only did he have to contend with Delphine, he had to win Davena. She had come to him easily last night, but only because she expected to die soon.

"And here I thought finding you and the lovely

Davena naked would erase that frown."

Beau's eyes snapped open to find Christian at the table with a mug of coffee in one hand and a slice of strawberry cake in the other. "What are you doing back so early?"

"Marshall came by the clinic. We chatted for a bit, and then he called the doc. I've been home for a couple of hours."

"You should've woken me," Beau said crossly as he stalked to the fridge and yanked open the door.

Christian swallowed his bite. "And ruin such a nice picture the two of you made? Not a chance. Tell me you didn't leave her to wake up alone?"

"Of course I didn't," Beau said and threw him a glare over his shoulder. "You're such an ass."

Christian screwed up his face. "Aren't you supposed to be in a glorious mood after a night in a woman's arms, especially a woman like Davena."

Beau inhaled, and then slowly released it. "I'm making her breakfast."

"Be careful with her, Beau. She'll slip through your fingers if you're not watching. She's used to being on her own."

Christian's words only tightened that niggle of worry at the back of his mind. "She has her sister to bury."

"And a psychopath to stay away from."

Beau grabbed the carton of eggs, milk, and grated cheese. "I don't plan to let her out of my sight again."

~ ~ ~

Davena smelled the eggs cooking and briefly thought about remaining, but she knew if she stayed, Delphine would come for her and kill all the Chiassons when she did.

The Chiassons were good people, and Beau...he was the best. He was the kind of man women prayed they would find, the kind of man who could smile and melt the stoutest of hearts.

The kind of man Davena had always yearned for.

The kind of man who needed to stay alive.

Davena slipped out the front door before she changed her mind.

~ ~ ~

He was a fool. A complete and utter fool.

Beau angrily shoved his hair out of his face as he stood in the office, staring down at the perfectly folded blanket that lay on the arm of the couch. A blanket that an hour earlier had been wrapped around Davena's lovely body.

The entire house was being searched for her, but he knew she was gone. Was it because she didn't trust him? Didn't she know a Chiasson didn't make a promise unless they could deliver on it?

"She's not in the house," Lincoln said as he stormed into the study. "Why did she leave?"

Ava was right on his heels. "You know why. Delphine."

"She said Delphine didn't have to enter the house to get to her," Beau said. "That's why she left. To protect us."

God, why hadn't he realized that sooner? If it had been anyone but Davena he would've comprehended that fact instantly. His mind was in constant turmoil where Davena was concerned.

Beau turned to face his brother and Ava and spotted the rest walking toward the doorway. He waited until everyone was gathered before he said, "If we're going to save Davena, we need to look for Delphine."

"Right, because that's so easy," Christian said.

Vincent frowned at him. "We know who we're looking for now. It's a small town with few places for her to hide."

"Yeah, but many small communities in which to do it," Lincoln pointed out.

Christian rubbed the back of his neck. "So much for staying away from the house once we found who we were after. She knows now."

Ava lifted a finger to get Beau's attention. "We'll get to that in a moment. What about Davena?"

"She knows I'll come looking for her. She'll stay hidden waiting for Delphine." Which would allow Beau time to find the priestess first if all went according to plan.

Vincent guessed his strategy and shook his head, baffled. "You really think Delphine will talk to you."

"What?" Christian yelled looking from Vincent to Beau. "Have you lost your fucking mind, Beau?"

Lincoln's smile was sad as he said, "No. He's

found his woman."

"I hate to bring this up," Olivia said, a forlorn look on her face. "Maman said someone would get hurt from this family. Beau, if you go looking for Delphine, that could end up being you."

Beau wiped a hand across his mouth. "Possibly."

He walked through the five of them and hurried upstairs to change. The clock had once more been set against them, but this time he knew who he had to save and who he was fighting against. That put the odds in his favor – slightly.

But Chiassons had been winning battles with less for generations. He wasn't going to give up because the odds were stacked against him. That's when a Chiasson excelled.

He dressed in record time, grabbing his shotgun on the way out of his room. When he reached the kitchen to go out the back door, everyone was waiting.

Olivia handed him a backpack with a warm smile. "There's food and water inside."

"As well as bandages and a change of clothes for both you and Davena," Ava added.

Beau drew both women in for a hug. "Thank you."

"Just bring her back," Ava said as Olivia dabbed at her eyes.

Beau then faced his brothers. "I have to do this alone."

"As if we'd allow that," Vincent stated.

Christian slapped him on the back as he walked

past him. "We're splitting up and covering your scrawny ass, little brother."

Beau watched him walk out, and a moment later heard the roar of an engine. Beau turned his gaze to Lincoln and Vincent. "Don't interfere in whatever I do."

"We can't promise that," Lincoln said and rubbed his thumb over the hilt of his Bowie knife. "You're our brother."

Vincent gave a small nod. "We'll do our best."

It was all Beau was going to get. He walked out of the house to his truck. Behind the wheel, he sat there for a moment thinking of where he might find Delphine. Then he started the engine and drove away.

He looked in the rearview mirror as he drove down the long crepe myrtle lined drive. The plantation loomed large and white. It had always been his safe haven, and he wanted it to be Davena's.

When he reached the main road, Beau looked left. That would take him toward Crowley, but going right would bring him to Kaplan. There had been rumors recently of Voodoo growing in the town. It seemed like the perfect place to look for Delphine.

Beau turned right. The knot that had been in his stomach for days had let up the previous night, but it was back with a vengeance, and had been since he was in the middle of cooking.

It wasn't long before he reached Kaplan and slowed. There wasn't the normal traffic for a

Sunday. Driving the streets wasn't going to get him anywhere. He needed to make himself accessible.

Beau pulled over at the local diner and parked. He glanced at his shotgun. Carrying it wasn't an option, and neither was trying to hide it. Fortunately, he had some throwing knives on him just in case. Not that any of it would matter if Delphine decided to kill him.

He hid his shotgun underneath the seat and got out of the truck. As he closed his door, he spotted Christian's blue truck across the street, and Lincoln's black truck down the street, just coming to a stop.

Beau turned around and came face to face with a black man as tall and thickly muscled as an oak. His midnight eyes were emotionless and trained on him.

"Delphine will see you," he said in an eerily deep voice. Then he turned and walked away.

Beau hesitated for a second before he fell in step behind the big man. Most likely he was walking to his death. At the very least, it was a trap. And yet he kept going.

The small town fell behind them as they crossed rice fields and pastures. Beau could see a copse of trees ahead, and just as he expected, that's where they stopped.

The big man pointed to an overturned bucket for Beau to sit on. Beau looked around at the bare earth. There were bones scattered around a banked fire along with a recently killed copperhead snake.

Beau counted at least ten men and women.

Some were hiding behind trees while others sat out in the open staring at him. He rested his arms on his legs and slowly looked around for some sign of Delphine.

Fifteen minutes went by excruciatingly slowly without a single word being spoken since he had arrived. He leaned back against the pine behind him and caught a flash of white through the trees.

A moment later Delphine stepped into the clearing. Her skin was a deep mocha, her eyes as black as pitch. She wore a white flowing skirt and shirt, and white material was wrapped around her head, hiding her hair.

Beau had only caught a glimpse of her in the dark the night before, so he was wholly unprepared for her exquisite beauty. She wore no makeup, no jewelry, and yet eclipsed everything around her.

"I knew you would come," she said with a small smile.

Beau was taken aback by her lush voice. She wasn't anything like he'd expected. An old crone perhaps, but not the beauty before him. "How did you know?"

"Because of Davena. You care for her."

"I do." There was no point in trying to lie. "Why do you want to kill her? Just because her mother went against you?"

Delphine's smile widened. "Because she's mine."

CHAPTER SIXTEEN

Davena sat in the rented house staring off into nothing. The house was particularly quiet without the constant chatter of Delia or the fighting. She kept waiting for her sister to come through the door with some argument about something trivial as she usually did, but Delia didn't come barging in. How could she when she was lying in a cold morgue?

Davena's throat tightened when she thought about the funeral. It wasn't right that Delia wouldn't be buried next to their parents – even though there was already a grave there.

It had been morbid, but Delia had made her sneak into the graveyard three years after their mother was killed to see their graves. Davena had been more interested in saying farewell to her mother, and she hadn't cared that the world thought her and Delia were already dead.

Now Delia would have a second grave, just as she would.

Davena wondered if her death would be as painful as Delia's. She hoped it was quick, but more than that, she prayed that Beau didn't witness it.

She wasn't stupid enough to believe he would let her leave. It wasn't in his genes. He would look for her in the hopes that he could save her. If she had a chance, hopefully she could talk Delphine into not harming the Chiassons.

If she got the chance to talk to Delphine. It was such a huge *if* that it was laughable. Her mother and Delia hadn't had that chance. What made her think she could?

Davena looked down at her hands. She had used magic last night. She realized that while she watched Beau sleep. She hadn't even known she could do it, but spells of Hoodoo from her mother filled her mind without her even trying.

Delia had brought Delphine to town by doing Hoodoo. It only made sense that Delphine would find her if she did the same. Davena stood and closed her eyes as she began to ward the house and those next to it against supernatural fire.

That should be enough to let Delphine know she wasn't hiding. Then Davena went to the drawer in the kitchen that held the knives and pulled out the biggest and two smaller ones. She took them to the table and began to mark them with a Hoodoo symbol to empower them with magic.

She wouldn't hide in the house like her mother, or be fool enough to try and face off against the priestess with her magic like Delia. She stood, hiding the knives in her shorts. No, Davena had another plan altogether.

~ ~ ~

Beau knew by Delphine's throaty laugh that she found his surprised expression funny. He composed himself quickly. "Yours? How is Davena yours?"

Delphine clasped her hands together in front of her and grinned while she waited for the big black male to lift a rather hefty piece of tree trunk from its place on one side of the clearing to set it in front of Beau.

She smiled seductively at the male and then sank gracefully onto the makeshift seat. "I'll tell you all about Davena if you answer me one question."

"Ask," he said, even though he knew it was going to be something he didn't want to answer.

"Would you die for her?"

He thought Delphine might ask if he loved Davena. He hadn't expected the question he got. "She doesn't deserve what has happened to her."

"That's not for you to decide," Delphine said, her black eyes going hard as her smile vanished. "I asked a question. I expect an answer."

The Chiassons were charged with keeping the people of the parish safe – in any way possible. He cared deeply for Davena, so deeply it might even be love. Every night they hunted, the Chiassons put their lives on the line, ready to die to save others. How would dying for Davena be any different?

"I would if I knew she would be free of you,"

he finally answered.

Delphine inhaled, her chest expanding. "A deal is a deal. You answered my question. Now I will tell you the story that only one other knew – Babette Arcineaux."

Beau waited for her to continue, each second that ticked by with silence grating on his nerves until he wanted to shout with it. That wasn't how to deal with Delphine, however. It took more finesse, more tact.

"Her mother couldn't conceive," Delphine said. "They tried unsuccessfully for years. They couldn't adopt, nor could they afford in vitro fertilization. After years of flaunting her Hoodoo in my face, Babette had the nerve to walk into my place."

He was riveted with the story. Beau couldn't imagine the nerve it took for Babette to see Delphine. "She wanted you to help her conceive," he guessed.

Delphine nodded. "I always knew she would want something from me someday, but it wasn't until she came to me that I knew what it would be."

"You helped her."

"I did." Delphine smiled secretly as she glanced away. "With one condition. I told her she would have more than one child. In exchange for my help, she had to agree that one of the children would be mine to raise in the Voodoo religion to take my place leading my followers someday."

Beau slowly leaned forward. "Davena."

"Davena," she repeated. She reached out her

hand and ran her long fingernail over his hand. "There were two spells that night. The first, Babette was witness to and included in. The second occurred long after she left. I gave some of my own power coursing in my veins to one of the children. I thought it might have been Delia."

"Because she was first?"

"She was conceived that very night, but no," Delphine said and caressed languidly up his arm. "It was her desire to know all there was to know of Voodoo and Hoodoo that made me think it was her. Then Davena caught my attention. She didn't care about what her mother did, and yet power filled her so fully she practically shone with it. Why do you think everyone always flocked to her?"

Beau tried to ignore her fingers as they reached his chest and then began to wander downward. "Because she's beautiful and good."

"Did you see how she put out my fire? No one has been able to do that before," Delphine said as she leaned closer. "No one."

"You fear her."

"She is part of me. I don't fear her, I love her. I came for her that night in Algiers, but Babette refused. That's why she died. I didn't know until it was too late that Davena was in there. I could have killed Delia right then, but I let both girls go. For six years, I've tracked their every movement."

Beau grabbed her hand right before she reached his cock. He slowly pulled her hand away. "Why come now?"

"Delia all but dared me, and it is past time that

Davena take her place beside me."

"So you're not here to kill Davena?"

Delphine yanked her hand from his grasp and smiled tightly. "No. However, I am prepared to use any incentive I came to...persuade...her to leave with me."

"You mean you're prepared to kill me and whoever else you need to," Beau guessed.

"I would so hate to end as fine a specimen as you are, Beau Chiasson, but if you don't help me I'll do just that *after* I make you watch while I kill your family. Including your sister."

Beau didn't think he could hate anyone as much as he did Delphine. There wasn't a doubt in his mind that Delphine wouldn't hesitate to do exactly as she claimed. "What do you want me to do?"

"Go to Davena. She wants a battle that I'd like to avoid."

"Can you blame her? She watched you kill her mother and sister, and she knows you killed her father."

Delphine threw back her head and laughed. "I didn't kill her father. That was done in retaliation after one of Babette's Hoodoo spells countering my hex failed. The woman's husband died, so she took Babette's."

"Why not come after you?"

"Everyone knows better."

Beau had come expecting to bargain for Davena's life. Instead, he was going to have to decide whether to convince Davena to go with Delphine to save his family.

Or sacrifice his family for her.

"Davena is at her house. You have a difficult choice," Delphine said as she stood and cupped his face. "I hope you make the right one, *mon cher*."

As one, the rest of the group rose and followed Delphine into the trees leaving Beau alone. He didn't wait around to see if anyone would come back. He was half way back to Kaplan when he saw his brothers waiting for him next to a fence. Beau didn't stop as he reached them. Delphine hadn't given him a time limit, but he didn't want to test her.

"So that was Delphine," Linc said as they fell into step beside him.

Beau gave a nod.

Vincent glanced at him. "We didn't get close enough to hear what she said, but she's stunning."

Christian let out a whistle in agreement. "If I didn't know how messed up she was in the head, I'd want her in my bed for a night."

"What did she want?" Lincoln asked.

Beau halted so quickly his brothers had taken several steps ahead of him. They stopped and turned to him. He looked at each of them, and his decision was made. "To make a long story short, Davena has Delphine's power. Babette couldn't have children, so she went to Delphine. The bargain was that one of the children would eventually take Delphine's place."

"Fuck, but that's messed up," Christian said.

Vincent smoothed back the hair in the queue at the base of his neck. "Agreed. So she's not here to kill Davena, but to bring her back to New Orleans?"

Beau grimly nodded. "It's why Babette was killed. Delphine came for Davena that night. She's known all along where the sisters have been."

"And Delia?" Christian asked. "Why kill her?"

"Delphine said Delia called her out, so to speak," Beau explained.

Fury laced Lincoln's face. "And no one can go against her."

"Exactly." Beau let out a long breath. "I have to convince Davena to go with her."

Christian grunted. "The hell you do."

"If I don't, she'll make me watch as all of you die, then she'll kill me."

Vincent's gaze caught his. "Our lives for Davena's."

"Essentially."

Christian shook his head and turned away. "Now do y'all understand why I'll never allow myself to be attached to a woman?"

"Shut up," Lincoln told Christian. He then turned his attention to Beau. "We're not defenseless. We can take care of ourselves."

"Not against the likes of her." Beau flattened his lips as he recalled something Davena had said the night before. "Davena said Delphine never lets something she wants go easily. She hasn't forgotten Ava or Jack, or what our cousins did to her."

Vincent let out a string of curses and began to pace. "They didn't capture her. She let them."

"That's my guess," Beau said.

Christian faced them again, his thumbs hooked in his belt loops. "What are you going to do?"

Beau looked to where his truck was parked feeling helpless and furious. "I'm going to find Davena."

"We'll come with you," Lincoln said.

Beau stopped him with a hand on his shoulder. "Go home, Linc. You too, Vin. Go to your women. Christian, make sure they get there and stay there."

"You want us to just leave you?" Christian asked.

Beau glanced at the ground. "I don't trust Delphine. You all stand the best chance at the house. I'll feel better knowing all of you are there waiting for me."

"If you don't come home, I'm going to kick your ass," Vin said before dragging him close for a hug.

Beau smiled as Vincent pounded on his back and quickly released him. He said brief farewells to Christian and Lincoln then headed to his truck.

CHAPTER SEVENTEEN

Davena found Delia's bag sitting on the bed. Somehow, she knew that Marshall had brought the car back as well as Delia's things. She unzipped the bag and peeked inside. Sitting right on top was a journal. Delia had written in it occasionally during their six years together. It seemed wrong to look inside it, but Davena reached for it anyway.

To read something of her sister's, and have that one last connection was too great to pass up. So Davena opened it and flipped through the pages chock full of Delia's handwriting. Emotion, thick and choking rose up in Davena when she found the last entry. Davena hastily swallowed and began to read.

September 3rd, Crowley

Davena still hasn't guessed what I have planned, and I'm so thankful for it. I have to do this for her. It's the only way she'll be able to stop looking over her shoulder. I'm hoping with everything that I learned from Mom, it will be enough to take on Delphine.

Even if it isn't, I can't sit back and do nothing anymore. I don't want to leave Davena, but I have to. She's all I have in the world, and it's time I stepped up as the eldest and took care of her as she's always taken care of me.

I just hope she forgives me for leaving. It's the only way I can carry out my plan. If she knows, she'll stop me, and I'm scared enough that I'd probably let her.

If she thinks I've left, it gives me the chance I need. And I know the perfect place to draw Delphine out. It's the animal clinic. It's near water, which will help strengthen what powers I have.

Besides, it's what Mom would've done.

Davena reread the passage three more times, each time more difficult than the last, bringing emotions she didn't want to feel because they frightened her so, overwhelmed her.

She jerked and nearly dropped the journal at the sound of a knock. Davena spun around and hastily walked into the living room. She glanced outside to see a silver truck.

"Beau," she whispered.

How had he found her? It didn't matter. He couldn't be there. She had to get rid of him quickly because he was her weakness.

Davena opened the door, the journal still in hand. His brilliant blue eyes locked on hers, and they held such understanding that a crack formed in the wall around her heart. Her vision swam as tears gathered and swiftly fell down her cheeks. There were no words as Beau stepped inside and drew her against him.

She clung to him, the tears she hadn't been able

to shed the night before coming in a torrent. Davena couldn't have stopped them if she tried. All the years of barely surviving, living in fear, and pretending life was better than it was came pouring out.

Beau's strong arms lifted her up and carried her to the couch where he sat down and held her tight. Davena didn't know how long they sat in silence as he let her cry. Even when the tears had dried, she didn't move. She was drained, emotionally and mentally. He moved her hair out of her face and kissed her forehead.

"Marshall brought Delia's things," Davena said finally. "I found her journal."

"Ah," Beau murmured.

Davena squeezed her eyes closed as she felt more tears coming. "The last time we spoke, we argued."

"She loved you, and she knew you loved her. You were family. It's what families do."

"Delphine will come for me today. I don't want you near when it happens."

He took a deep breath and slowly released it. "I'm not leaving."

Davena sat up and looked at him. She sniffed and rubbed her nose that she knew had turned red as it always did when she cried. "I left the plantation to keep this away from you and your family."

"It doesn't matter. Delphine wants it otherwise."

Davena felt the room spin around her. "What?"

"First, I want you to know that I was coming for you regardless."

"Just say it," Davena said nervously. That gnawing, gaping feeling that threatened to swallow her whole was growing bigger by the second. She instinctively knew that whatever Beau was about to say was going to change her world – and not for the better.

He pulled her against him for a quick kiss, and then looked into her eyes. "Tell me you know I was coming for you."

"I knew you would try to find me," she conceded. It was who Beau was. She understood that, which is why she had prayed he wouldn't know where to find her.

His eyes briefly closed. "Delphine isn't coming to kill you, Davena. She's coming to claim you."

"I'm sorry. That sounded like you just said she wasn't going to kill me after she murdered my sister and my parents," Davena said as she slid off Beau's lap.

It bothered her more than she wanted to admit that he didn't try to keep her against him.

He sat forward and ran a hand down his weary face. "Delphine claims she didn't kill your father. She says that one of your mother's clients was seeking revenge when Babette's counterspell against one of Delphine's hexes didn't work, and because she had lost her husband, she decided to take your mother's."

"And you believe her?"

"She has no reason to lie. She takes credit for

every life she's taken."

Davena didn't think her legs could hold her much longer, and it was obvious the surprises were going to keep coming. "Why does she want me?"

"Your mother went to her when she couldn't get pregnant. Delphine agreed to help your mother conceive, but only with the understanding that one of the children would be Delphine's to train in Voodoo to take her spot as priestess one day. Delphine mixed her own power into the spell."

Davena thought of all the times Delphine had sought her out whether to speak to her, or just to watch her. Now she understood Delphine's interest. It sickened her that she was part of someone so evil and that her mother had agreed to such a thing just to have children.

Beau saw her sway, and was on his feet with his arms around her before her legs could give out. He sat her on the sofa beside him, holding her ice-cold hand in his.

On his way to see her, he had thought of a thousand different ways to tell her to go with Delphine in order to save his family. It was the right thing to do because everyone would remain alive.

Then he realized that Davena could be carrying his child. It had been a reckless thing they did having unprotected sex, but he couldn't find any regret in anything he had done with Davena. The possibility of a child only brought to the forefront the reality that by sending Davena to Delphine, he was going against his family's code.

Then Davena had opened her door. He had seen the remorse and sadness in her spring green eyes, and it had firmed his resolve to help her. His family would take care of themselves. It was his duty to protect Davena at all costs — even if it meant his own life.

"My parents wanted a child so desperately they made a deal with Delphine? What kinds of people do that?"

He didn't know how to answer that because he'd never been in that position. "The fact is, your mother did it. The night your mother died, Delphine had come for you. Babette refused to give you up."

"So Delphine killed her," Davena said. "And nearly killed me and Delia."

"Delphine claims not to have known you were in there initially, but when she found out, she kept the fire from reaching you. She knew you and Delia escaped, but she let you go."

Davena gave a shake of her head. "Why would she do that?"

"She says to give you time, but I suspect there's more to it. She's always known where you were. Delphine was going to come for you soon, but Delia challenged her."

"I'm going to kill that bitch."

Beau gathered her other hand with the first and rubbed his thumb along her knuckles. "You have the power to face her, but I don't want you to."

Her gaze settled on him, anger clearing them of sorrow. "Why?"

"Because I don't want you to die. I care about you, Davena, even though I tried hard not to."

She looked down at their joined hands. "Delphine wanted you to talk me into going with her, didn't she?"

"Yes." Beau wasn't going to lie to her. If Davena was going to make a life-changing decision, she needed to know all there was to know. "I'm not going to though. There has to be another way."

Davena chuckled dryly and looked at him. "There's not. Delphine always gets what she wants. She wants me. If she doesn't get me, she'll kill me and everyone around…" She trailed off, her eyes going wide. "She threatened your family, didn't she?"

This was one thing he wanted to lie about. "It's what people like her do, but we're used to it. My brothers are readying themselves."

"And Ava and Olivia?"

"With my brothers. They're a lot safer than we are."

Davena frowned. "And your sister?"

Beau's gut twisted just thinking about it. He hadn't been able to get ahold of Riley, but he had left several messages. They had believed her safe in Austin, but with her being so far away from any family, there was no one there to help her.

"Oh, God," Davena whispered and hung her head. She sniffed loudly. "Delphine will keep killing unless I go with her. I've lost my sister. There's no reason for you to lose yours."

Beau cupped her face and lifted her chin to

look into her eyes. Her golden mane of hair hung around her shoulders, and her eyelashes were still spiky from her tears. "You don't belong with Delphine."

"Your family has been so good to me." She reached up and put her hand atop his. "You protected me, but now it's my turn to protect you."

"Davena, no."

"I won't see you or your family hurt. You see, Beau Chiasson, I care about you, too."

He started to speak when his eyes all of a sudden grew heavy. No matter how he fought, he couldn't stop his lids from closing. That's when he knew Davena was using magic on him. He tried to call her name as his eyes closed.

Davena carefully laid Beau back on the couch. She stroked his face and the thick whiskers along his jaw. "I would've shared my life with you. I would have done anything for your love. Stay safe, Beau. You have a full life ahead of you continuing to save those in the parish."

She stood and picked up Delia's journal that had been dropped sometime during their conversation. Davena looked back at Beau sleeping so peacefully. He would be angry when he woke, but she had to do something.

If she hadn't, he would do something foolish like stand with her against Delphine, and she couldn't allow that. She loved him too much for that.

Fresh tears came as she realized that she did love him. Deeply, intently.

Totally.

It was for him that gave her the strength to walk from the house and face her nemesis. There was evil in the bayous, evil that wouldn't stop until she had what she came for.

Davena was going to give Delphine something unexpected, something the Voodoo priestess would never see coming.

CHAPTER EIGHTEEN

Beau came awake after a vicious slap to his face. He jerked upright, his fist swinging.

"Son of a bitch," he heard a male growl angrily.

Beau blinked several times, trying to get his eyes to focus. He was so tired he couldn't form a coherent thought. Somehow he got to his feet, knocking into something heavy, and lifted his fists.

"It might help if you opened your damn eyes."

He frowned because he recognized the voice. It took him a moment, but he finally placed it. Marshall Ducet. What was Marshall doing in Davena's house?

Davena.

Beau's eyes cracked open as clarity hit him like a tidal wave. He wouldn't have fallen asleep on his own. That meant Davena had put him in that state? "Where is she?"

"I don't know," Marshall said as he rubbed his jaw. "You've got a hell of a left hook, even for someone asleep."

Beau plopped back down onto the couch and gave his head a shake to clear it more. "I wasn't sleeping."

"Really? What do you call that?"

"Magic," Beau grumbled. "Why are you here?"

"After your call to find Davena's house, I thought you might want some help."

Right. Beau wasn't fooled. "Who called you?"

Marshall sighed loudly. "I was on my way here when Christian rang. It's a good thing I gave my number to everyone last night. Did Delphine get Davena?"

"No." It was much worse than that. "She went to Delphine so my family would be left alone."

Marshall rested his hand on the butt of his 9mm. "Brave girl."

"Foolish is more like it. We could've thought of something."

"She knows Delphine. Even I know better than to mess with the likes of Delphine."

Beau looked at his watch. "She's been gone about fifteen minutes. Did you see Davena on your way here?"

"No, but she'd likely stay off the roads for just such a thing."

"I know." Beau got to his feet and started for the door. "I've got to stop her."

"Have you ever thought that maybe she's doing the right thing?"

Beau halted with his hand on the doorknob. He looked over his shoulder at the deputy. "I know she's not. She's a good person who doesn't need to be anywhere near Delphine."

"Davena is old enough to make her own decisions."

"I'm not losing her!"

Beau looked away after his outburst and rested his forehead against the door. His nerves were stretched taut, his heart racing with dread and fear.

It was exactly the thing he had never wanted to experience. He'd known how easy it would be to fall for Davena, which is why he hadn't pursued her.

Fate, destiny, or whatever you wanted to call it had put her in his path regardless of what either of them wanted. There had been a part of him missing that he hadn't even realized until she was near and he felt whole. Then it was crystal clear that she was what was lacking.

How did he go through life knowing she was out of his reach? How could he face each day thinking about her learning all of Delphine's ways?

How could he survive without her in his arms?

"You love her."

Beau frowned. "I protect people."

"Especially someone you've fallen in love with," Marshall persisted.

"I know better than to fall in love with anyone."

Marshall chuckled, his boots sounding on the wood floor as he walked closer. "Good luck with that train of thought. Anyone with eyes can see the two of you have something special. Whether it's love now or not, it's extraordinary and shouldn't be carelessly tossed aside."

Beau straightened and looked at him. "I'm so scared of losing her that I don't know what to do."

"Yes you do." Marshall moved him aside and opened the door. "You've been doing this your whole life. You've known what to do this entire time."

Beau looked outside to see the sun shining bright. It seemed wrong to have such a beautiful day when everything was falling apart.

He could wallow in self-pity, or he could remember that he was a Chiasson. Marshall was right. He had been hunting since he was a small boy. The only thing different was that he was older and more experienced at hunting evil.

"I don't know if this will bleed over into the public. You need to get to town."

Marshall walked past him. "Nice try. I'm coming with you."

"The hell you are," Beau said as he stormed out of the house, slamming the door behind him.

"Your family isn't with you, and you're going to need backup."

"Not from someone that doesn't know what's going on."

"Don't forget I lived in New Orleans for years, Beau. I dealt with Delphine and all the other craziness like werewolves, vampires, and witches that abound in that city. I'm not a novice."

Beau looked to the sky for patience before he sighed. Marshall was going to go with him no matter what. Beau could use him to his advantage.

"Fine, but you'll have to stay out of sight. If she gets wind that you're there, she'll kill you in an instant."

"I'm interested in living, so I'll stay hidden."

Beau walked to his truck. "I must be out of my mind."

"How do you know where Davena is?"

"I don't, but I know she'll get as far from the city and people as she can. That doesn't leave too many places."

Beau got into his truck and glanced in his rearview mirror to see Marshall already in his own car with the engine started. He started the truck and put it in gear.

"Hold on, Davena. I'm coming."

~ ~ ~

Sweat ran down Davena's face and back. Her thin, turquoise shirt was stuck to her, and her denim shorts only made her hotter. She was squinting painfully in the sun, and the hair sticking to her neck and face was making her itch.

But she ignored all of it as she concentrated on what was to come. If she did have some of Delphine's power within her, then that made her one of a handful who had the ability to stand against the priestess.

A desperate few had dared to stand against Delphine, and every one of them had died. Davena had expected death, but after what Beau imparted, she was willing to bet her very soul that Delphine wouldn't be so hasty to kill her.

Davena swiped at the tears that began. She hadn't been able to shed one yesterday, but today she couldn't stop. She cried for Delia, for the happiness she had found with Beau then lost, and the love she held for him that would never be fulfilled.

She continued walking through the pasture. Davena had lost count of the fences she had climbed over. She was getting further and further from the city, but there were still a few houses nearby.

She walked for another thirty minutes before she stopped and looked around. The nearest house was just a dot on the horizon, and only a few trees were scattered in the field.

Davena went to the nearest tree and sighed once she was under the shade. Now all she had to do was wait.

~ ~ ~

Beau sped down the back roads. He had already been to two of the five places Davena could have gone. The third was just up ahead. He slowed long enough to grab his binoculars and do a quick scan.

His lips flattened when he didn't see a sign of her. Beau tossed aside the binoculars and sped away. The knot he was accustomed to feeling was gone, leaving an empty void once more.

If he didn't find Davena, that emptiness would never be filled again. He would be vacant, hollow the rest of his days. That thought pushed him harder.

He stomped on the accelerator. Marshall was right behind him at all times. With two more spots to check, Beau had to decide which direction to go in when he came to a stop sign. He looked first one way and then the other. If he made the wrong decision, he could lose Davena forever.

Beau slammed his hand down on the steering wheel in frustration. "Come on!" he yelled at himself.

He had known Davena was in trouble, had known exactly where to go to help her. Now that she was in over her head he felt nothing.

"I have to find her," he said and closed his eyes.

It took three tries to clear his head of everything and focus on Davena. He thought of her courage, of the pure energy flowing through her. He thought of her lips and her cries of pleasure as he filled her.

Beau's eyes snapped open. He turned to the left and pushed the truck past a hundred for the next few miles. Then he turned off down a dirt road, his truck bouncing all over the place.

He slammed on the brakes, skidding to a stop when he came to an empty field. By the time he got out of his truck, Marshall was beside him, a rifle in hand. They met at the fence, each man looking over the terrain.

"She's here," Beau said.

Marshall checked the rifle. "There isn't much cover."

"Looks like you're going to have to do some crawling, deputy."

Marshall gave him a droll look. "Don't look so pleased with yourself."

"It might be character building."

"You sound like my drill sergeant."

"Military, huh? Which branch?" Beau asked.

Marshall loaded more bullets into the rifle and then slung the strap over his shoulder. "Marines. Where are you headed?"

"There," Beau said and motioned to a tree off in the distance.

Marshall put his hand atop the fence and leapt over it. "I'll come up on the side."

"Remember, stay hidden," Beau said. "Delphine has a big man with her. He'll most likely be hidden, but he's never far behind."

"I know him," Marshall stated and headed off at a run, bent low.

Beau watched him for a moment before he put both hands on the fence and jumped over it. He landed on the other side and took the most direct path to the tree.

He hadn't seen any sign of Davena, but he trusted his instincts. They hadn't led him wrong about her before. She was somewhere out there waiting for Delphine.

A glance to the right and Beau briefly caught sight of Marshall He was moving quickly, covering twice as much ground. It gave Beau an idea.

He bent low and started jogging. If Davena saw him before he reached her, she would more than likely do something to stop him, and Beau wasn't going to allow that. He was there to help whether she wanted it or not.

The next time Beau looked for Marshall, he couldn't find the deputy. Beau hoped he was as good as he appeared, because it might well come down to Marshall killing Delphine to end all of this.

When Beau was halfway to the tree he stopped and dropped to his knees. The grass was tall enough to hide him, but wasn't nearly enough cover. He saw movement by the tree and recognized Davena.

The relief left him almost dizzy. He didn't allow himself to celebrate quite yet, though. Just as he was about to continue on, he caught sight of someone else walking toward Davena.

"Delphine," Beau muttered angrily.

CHAPTER NINETEEN

Davena was strangely calm. The serenity that overtook her was almost unnerving. She couldn't pinpoint exactly when it occurred, but it was sometime during her walk that morning.

Perhaps it was because of the certainties she now knew. That she wouldn't let any harm come to Beau or his family. That she wasn't going anywhere with Delphine. That she was willing to die to stop Delphine.

Maybe it was because she felt the power flowing through her, a power she had pretended not to sense for years. That power was formidable and violent.

Whatever the reason, Davena was ready to face her nemesis. So when she caught sight of Delphine coming toward her, she simply closed her eyes and relaxed. She had to calm her mind, to find a place deep within herself to store all of her fears and hopes and dreams.

A place to put her time with Beau and the love

that blossomed in her heart.

Because Delphine would use any means necessary to get what she wanted. She would try to hurt anyone connected with Davena, and Delphine would exploit her love for Beau.

Davena couldn't let words anger her or cause her to react quickly. She had to be completely withdrawn from everything and everyone. She had to overlook that her mother had been sliced before her eyes. She had to disregard that Delia had been murdered the day before. And she had to forget all about Beau.

Casting those sweet memories of Beau and the safety his arms provided aside was the hardest thing she had ever done. When the last one was tightly shut away, Davena continued to keep her eyes closed.

She could hear Delphine's steps now, knew she was close. Delphine might be powerful, but she was also predictable. She liked to see the fear in people's eyes. More importantly, she wanted Davena.

That was Delphine's weakness. It would be that weakness that Davena exploited as Delphine had exploited countless others.

Davena let several minutes tick by long after Delphine reached her. She knew the priestess was growing angry, and it was just what Davena wanted. She would be composed while Delphine was anything but.

When Davena finally opened her eyes, Delphine was standing about ten feet from her, just under the shade of the tree. She looked Delphine over in her all white clothes and couldn't figure out what she had been so afraid of for all those years.

"So," Delphine said in her husky voice. "Beau convinced you. I wondered if he would choose his family or you. Looks like his family means more to him."

Davena remained sitting against the tree as if she weren't facing a powerful Voodoo priestess. "He told me everything."

"Everything? Yes, I suppose he did. Why else would you be here but to protect him?"

Davena smiled. Next, Delphine would threaten Beau if she didn't immediately return to New Orleans with her. Time to shake things up a bit. "I'm here because he told me I have some of you within me."

There was a beat of silence, and a pleased look filled Delphine's black eyes. "That you do, *mon cher*. Without my power and magic, you wouldn't be here now."

"True. I have you to thank, then."

Delphine's eyes narrowed a fraction. "Appreciation? This I didn't expect."

"I'm alive because of you." Davena used the tree and got to her feet. "Did you think I'd be angry because you killed my mother and sister?"

"Yes."

Davena bit back a grin. "I'm not angry. I see now that you were clearing my path so I would see nothing but you."

"Is that so?"

"Yes."

Delphine threw back her head and laughed. "Oh, Davena, you have more of me than I realized. You might have your mother's coloring and your father's eyes, but the rest of you is all me. If I'd known, I'd have taken you when you were just a child."

A thread of fury began to grow, but Davena quickly stamped it out. "Why not have children of your own? Why give me what could have passed to your own child?"

"My ability to have children was taken from me when I was too young to even know what was going on. Do you remember the name Lisette?"

"I know that name well. She was the priestess before you."

"Yes, and she took my ability to have children into herself."

This was a story Davena had never heard. "Why not take it back?"

"That wasn't possible, but I got my revenge."

Davena could well imagine how, but Delphine would expect her to ask nonetheless. "How?"

"I waited until Lisette was in the middle of labor with her third child. I had been brought in to help, along with two others. When it was close to the babe arriving, I brought in her two other children, both girls, and slit their throats as she watched. The women with me held down Lisette's hands as I cut her stomach and pulled the babe from her womb."

"You killed the babe then," Davena guessed.

Delphine's smile grew. "I did. Lisette grew enraged and tried to curse me, but I killed her before she could complete the spell."

"And then you took over."

"I was the youngest priestess ever in New Orleans."

Davena looked away. "You got your revenge and the throne, so to speak. I wouldn't think you'd be giving up your position as priestess anytime soon."

"I won't, but you need to be there to learn from me. The others need to see you, as well."

"You have no intention of turning over your position."

"Of course not. However, to keep others from stepping out of place, I need to pacify them, which means you'll come home with me."

"And if I'm not ready to go to New Orleans yet?" She wasn't about to tell Delphine that she would never return with her.

Delphine's eyes hardened a fraction. "You've had your time, Davena. I gave you all those years as you grew up. These past six you should've been by my side."

"Yeah, about that," she said and smoothed back her hair. "If you knew where I was at all times, why didn't you come and get me?"

Delphine hesitated a moment too long.

It was Davena's turn to smile. "Ah. You don't want me there, but you've spoken about me to all of your followers for so long that they want me in New Orleans now. You think I'm going to kill you as you did Lisette and take over."

"You don't have enough power for that yet."

"Yet," Davena repeated. "And you'll make sure I'm never quite there. You'll keep me under your thumb, to prove to your followers that they need you and only you. Tell me, can you live forever?"

Delphine took a step closer. "I can live far longer than you think."

"I believe you can do a great many things. You kill easily enough, and you are quick to curse and hex anyone you feel might be plotting against you. It must be exhausting."

Davena saw movement behind Delphine and spotted another form in all white. As he drew closer, Davena noticed the man was not only tall, but also hulking.

"That would be Joseph," Delphine said. "He is always near."

Davena still had a few moments alone with Delphine. "What's your plan?"

"You'll come with me or I'll kill Beau."

"Beau was certainly a nice way to pass the time."

Delphine's head cocked to the side as she asked, "You really think I'll fall for that?"

"If you've watched me all these years, how many times have I ever let a man close? How many have I dated for more than one night?"

"None," she answered sullenly.

"Beau Chiasson is no different from any of the others."

~ ~ ~

Beau hated the uncertainty he felt at Davena's words. He didn't know if she had played him, or if she was pulling one over on Delphine, and he was likely never to know.

He had managed to sneak up close enough before Delphine arrived. Davena had been so intent on her that she hadn't realized he was crawling close enough to the tree to hear her breathing.

The Davena he listened to was in complete control. There was little emotion coming through her voice, and though he couldn't see her from his position, he could only imagine she looked just as calm as she sounded.

"He believes otherwise," Delphine said. "He loves you."

Beau ignored the bite of fire ants on his hand. With one swipe, he raked them off and shifted out of the ant pile while he waited for Davena's response.

"Beau has no such interest in me. It was his way of attempting to allow me time to leave the area. He is dedicated to wiping the parish of people like us. He wants me gone, and you with me."

"You're lying." Delphine finished it off with a small chuckle. "It's so obvious that it's painful."

Beau wasn't sure what Davena's plan was, but he was going to be ready for anything.

"What's painful is you looking for a way to hurt me. You've already done it," Davena said in a soft voice. "You killed my mother and sister. There's no one left for you to threaten."

"I can kill every Chiasson with just a thought."

"Do it," Davena pressed. "All you'll do is send more hunters after you."

Delphine cackled. "You mean the LaRues? They're at my mercy. They may want me dead, but they'll never succeed."

Beau couldn't wait to share the information with his cousins. They would be curious to know that Delphine thought them nothing more than a nuisance.

"Let me save us both some time. You don't want me in New Orleans, and I don't want to be there."

"You're coming with me," Delphine said and fire rose in a roaring circle around the tree, the flames singeing the branches.

Beau ground his teeth together and stood so that his back was against the tree. The heat from the fire caused him to sweat more. The sweat fell into his eyes, stinging them until they watered.

"Kill me. I don't care," Davena said. "Perhaps I can hurry things along and take you with me."

No sooner had the words left her mouth than the whistle of wind swooped in. The wind swept the flames horizontally until there was a wall of fire spinning around them and rising higher than the tree.

There was no way Marshall would be able to help him now. Regardless, he had to try and kill Delphine. He just hoped Joseph wasn't inside the fire circle with them.

"Impressive," Delphine said.

"If I was trying to impress you, I'd have killed you." Davena moved, stepping on a pinecone.

"Then why the wind and this remarkable wind fire?"

Beau peeked around the tree to see Davena cross her arms over her chest.

"To show you that I have nothing else to lose," Davena replied.

"Is that right?" Delphine asked succinctly.

Beau pressed back against the tree as smoke surrounded him, alive, just as it had been in his dream. It wound around his feet and continued up his legs.

"I'm killing every Chiasson as we're standing here," Delphine continued.

"Lies."

"Is it?"

Beau could stand there and be smothered to death, or he could take his chance while he had it. He shifted, pushing against the smoke, withdrew one of the throwing knives from the belt at his waist, and took aim. The smoke was up to his chest now and moving faster.

If Delphine was right and there was smoke attacking the rest of his family, then everything rested with him. He took a deep breath to block the smoke that was now at his face. He let the knife fly, the blade spinning end over end as it headed toward Delphine.

He fell, the smoke knocking him sideways from

behind the tree as he threw a second knife. Delphine used her power to knock the blade meant for her away, but she wasn't able to stop the second, which embedded in Joseph's neck.

The big male fell backwards into the flames, his body engulfed instantly.

Delphine jerked her head to Beau, her eyes filled with hatred.

He glanced at Davena to see her examining the scar on her palm. Just as he thought he might be fighting Delphine alone, Davena's green eyes met his and she winked.

CHAPTER TWENTY

Davena couldn't believe that Beau was there. Her spell should've kept him asleep until just a few minutes ago. Long enough for her to get far enough away that he'd never know where to look.

She was also furious that he was there. The shock at seeing the blade come out of seemingly nowhere had kept her still. Then Beau had appeared. It had been almost comical watching Delphine easily bat away the knife, unaware that a second had been thrown at Joseph.

"I'll kill you for that," Delphine said menacingly to Beau.

That's when Davena saw the smoke covering him. From somewhere in her mind, the spell to stop it appeared. She quickly said the words and watched as it was sucked back into the wall of flames.

Beau sucked in huge mouthfuls of air as he hurriedly climbed to his feet. Davena reached for one of her hidden knives and stepped between

Delphine and Beau, her gaze locked on the priestess. "No, you won't. You're going to leave, and you're going to forget about this parish and everyone in it – including me."

"Not likely, *mon cher.*"

"One last chance, Delphine. Leave."

The priestess laughed, a red haze flaring in her eyes. Davena was knocked out of the way as a flash of flames came at her from the circle. She blinked and looked down at Beau. He had been the one to pull her aside, taking the fall as he did. Davena didn't have time to thank him or look for the knife that had been knocked out of her hand. She had to prove her point before they both died.

Davena got to her feet and confronted Delphine. "I did warn you."

"You can't compare to me," Delphine said with an evil grin.

Words filled Davena's mind – Hoodoo and Voodoo alike. It was the knowledge of her mother and the power of Delphine working and mixing together, mingling and blending to form a new power until Davena's entire body hummed with it.

All the while, Delphine was working her own magic, but it couldn't match what was inside Davena. A smile pulled at her lips because she knew she could kill Delphine with merely a thought.

"I'm not a killer," Davena said more to herself than Delphine.

The priestess smiled coldly. "That's why you're going to lose."

Davena cocked her head, and with a wave of her hand had Delphine hanging in midair. She thought it might be enough to stop whatever Delphine had in mind.

She should've known better.

Beau let out a bellow, his hands on his head as he fell to his knees. The look of excruciating pain on his face was almost enough for her to kill Delphine right then. If she did, how would she ever be able to look at herself in the mirror again, much less face Beau?

Davena turned back to Delphine to see the triumph in her eyes. "Enough."

"No!" Delphine bellowed.

It was the last straw for Davena. She moved Delphine back until the edge of her skirt touched the fire circle. Davena kept the fire from consuming Delphine's clothes, but only just.

Delphine's gaze jerked to her, comprehension dawning that Davena wasn't just a match for her, but more powerful as well. Several seconds ticked by before Beau fell forward on all fours, his head hanging and his breathing coming in great gasps.

Eventually, he looked up and gave a nod. Relief filled her so quickly Davena grew lightheaded. She pulled Delphine away from the fire and extinguished the flames on her skirt, but she kept her hanging in midair.

Beau slowly stood and came to stand beside her. Davena used that time to stop the wind and put out the fire altogether.

She walked closer to Delphine, her chin lifted.

"You have two choices. You can push me one more time, in which case I will kill you. You know I have the power to do it."

"And the second?" Delphine asked tightly.

"Leave. Joseph is dead. There's no one to know what really happened other than you. Tell them I'm dead. Tell them I don't have any power. I don't care what you say, but let them know that I will never come to take your place. I make my own destiny."

Delphine's black eyes slid to Beau. "With him?"

"With myself," Davena said. "No more running, no more being afraid. Make your choice, Delphine."

The priestess composed herself, the red fading from her eyes. "I will return to New Orleans."

Davena lowered Delphine back to the ground. She started to walk away when Davena called her name.

"One more thing," Davena said as she moved to stand nose-to-nose with the priestess. "You're anger is with me. Not with the Chiassons, and certainly not with the LaRues or anyone connected with either family. If any of them die under mysterious circumstances or has a curse put on them, I'll be coming for you. I will destroy you and your followers without a second thought or bothering to ask if it was you. Do you understand?"

Fury blazed in Delphine's gaze. "Perfectly."

Davena stepped back and let the priestess walk away. She remained prepared in case Delphine tried anything, and she stayed that way until the priestess was out of sight.

Then Davena sagged against the tree, Beau's arms coming around her to hold her up. She was afraid to look at him, afraid to know that he believed everything she had said to Delphine.

"That was...incredibly sexy," Beau said.

It was so unexpected that a laugh bubbled from Davena. She looked up at him, her throat clogging with emotion when she gazed into his bright blue eyes. "You were here the entire time?"

"Most of it. I arrived before Delphine and hid behind the tree. You were too focused on Delphine to notice."

"Beau, what I said —"

He nodded and interrupted her by saying, "I know."

"You do?"

His smile was slow and heart stopping. "I know you, Davena. I know you care about people and family. I knew you would go as far from the town as you could. And...I know you love me."

She was so stunned that she could only stare blankly at him. How did he know? She hadn't said anything to him about him.

Davena's mind halted when his hand slid to the back of her head and he took her lips in a sensual, savage kiss. Safely ensconced in Beau's embrace, she wrapped her arms around his neck and returned the kiss with fervor.

A new beginning had started for her, one with infinite possibilities.

Someone cleared their throat, breaking them

apart. She looked away as soon as her gaze landed on Marshall. Beau chuckled as the two shared smiles.

"You brought Marshall?" Davena asked in surprise.

Marshall grunted, though his smile was wide. "I didn't give him a choice, not that I did much good. That wall of fire thing kept me from seeing anything."

Davena had thought no one would see what she could do. She didn't want to be known as the freak of town. She tried to turn away, but Beau held her still.

"Don't hide what you are." Beau's tone was serious, as was the look on his face.

Marshall slung the rifle over his shoulder. "He's right, Davena. Embrace who you are because I think you'll find you fit in well here."

"As do you, deputy," she said with a grin.

Marshall gave a tip of his hat and turned on his heel. They watched him walk back to his car for long moments.

"So," Beau said. "Do you have plans for the night?"

She gave a shake of her head. "No, I'm free."

"What about the rest of your life?"

Davena bit her lip. "You barely know anything about me."

"We're going to remedy that starting tonight. You love me, remember?"

"I do." She licked her lips, suddenly incredibly nervous. Her courage came from the knowledge that Beau wouldn't still be beside her if he didn't care for her, as well. "What about you?"

His eyes twinkled with merriment. "What about me?"

"You know my feelings, but I don't know yours."

"Don't you," he whispered and pulled her tightly against him. "I've not hidden them from our first meeting. I can't, not when it comes to you."

She ran her fingers through his long hair and kissed him. "I've not had any kind of relationship in six years."

"Then we'll take it slow," he whispered. "You get to choose. Just promise you'll never leave. I need you, Davena. I love you."

"And I love you. I don't want to ever be without you."

"I'm a hunter. I'm gone most nights fighting evil."

Davena's heart swelled as she realized what a great man she had. "I'm very good at fighting evil myself, you know."

"Do I ever," he growled and turned them so he had her pinned against the tree.

EPILOGUE

One day later...

Beau slammed the truck door on Vincent and took Davena's hand. She was laughing along with Ava and Olivia.

"What?" Vincent said as he opened the door and got out of the truck. "All I said was that there was room enough in the house for everyone."

Christian groaned loudly. "For the love of God, Vin, let it go. Everyone wants their privacy, me included. I can't exactly walk around naked anymore."

"See?" Beau said with a hand out toward Christian as he looked between Vincent and Lincoln. "That right there. Yes, the house is plenty big enough, but there's no reason we all have to stay together."

Lincoln was laughing as he held up his hands for everyone to stop walking and quiet down. "All right. I see both sides. Vincent, you want everyone here, and I see that. However, I also understand Christian's and Beau's sides. They were going to talk to us about moving out before Davena came into the picture, so it's nothing new."

"Riiight," Vincent said grumpily. "You all are ganging up on me. Olivia, are you still on my side."

"Babe, I'm always on your side." She leaned up to kiss his cheek. "But I think everyone should get to choose."

Ava nodded quickly. "I agree with Olivia."

Vincent threw up his hands in defeat. "Wonderful."

"Wait," Lincoln said. "I wasn't finished."

Christian blew out a frustrated breath.

Lincoln threw him a nasty look. "I get that everyone needs their own space, but I agree with Vincent that everyone should stay here."

Beau laughed and looked down at Davena who wore a bright smile.

"Honey," Ava said. "I hate to tell you this, but that doesn't solve anything."

Lincoln pulled her against his side and slapped her on the ass. "If I could finish."

"By all means," Christian said cantankerously.

"There is plenty of land. Who says we can't build our own homes?" Lincoln suggested.

It was such a good idea that everyone looked around waiting for an argument. When none was made, Lincoln took a bow. "Thank you, thank you. I'm here all the time."

Christian slapped him on the back of the head. "Jerk off."

Laughter ensued as Lincoln chased Christian around to the back of the house. Everyone else followed in time to see Lincoln tackle him to the ground, then sit on top of him, his hands in the air.

Ava let out a long whistle and clapped. "Yay, baby!"

Beau stopped and frowned. "Do you smell that?"

"Smell what?" Olivia asked as she and Vincent halted beside him.

Davena sniffed the air. "It smells like apple pie."

"It does," Vincent agreed. He looked down at Olivia. "Is Maria here?"

Olivia was shaking her head even as Beau walked through the porch to the back door. Davena was right beside him, and the others were on his heels. He threw open the door and everyone piled into the kitchen.

A whirl of long, dark waves turned and smiled in welcome. "I made Momma's apple pie."

"Riley," Beau said with a shake of his head, but a smile nonetheless.

The shit storm was about to rain down for sure.

Look for the next story in the Chiasson series with their cousins, the LaRues in **MOON KISSED** – Coming November 10, 2014!

Until then, read on for the sneak peek at **BURNING DESIRE**, the third book in the Dark King series…

Dreagan Industries

Cork, Ireland
May

Pretending. Misleading. Mimicking.

Kiril and the rest of his brethren had been perfecting those acts since they sent their dragons away and set about blending in with the humans. They had honed their skills to a degree that only a handful of people in the entire world knew who they really were—Dragon Kings.

It had been difficult for the first millennia to pretend they weren't once rulers of the realm. After that, it became a habit, a way of life. What else was a Dragon King to do when the dragons were gone?

Kiril spent many centuries deep in his cave, asleep, hidden from the world and the shockingly easy way their reign had passed from legend to myth. Even then he wasn't free from his memories or the longing to be the dragon he was born to be.

No, in the dragon sleep, he relived the glorious time when the dragons ruled the Earth, when roars filled the air, and dragons were free to roam the skies, the ground, and even the waters as they wanted.

And then the humans came.

Kiril clenched his teeth together as he drove down the winding, narrow road toward Cork. He wasn't sure if he would ever be rid of his repugnance for them. He didn't blame all humans. After all, five of his fellow Kings had recently bound themselves to human females.

However, eons ago, it had been a human female who had made a vow to one of them, only to betray him and set in motion a war that could have destroyed them all. It was only the Kings banding together, and Constantine, the King of Kings, who came up with a solution—sending the dragons to another realm.

Kiril sped his sleek Sepang brown Mercedes SLS AMG Roadster along the winding roads with the top down and the wind whipping around him. It was the closest thing to flying that he could allow himself while remaining in Ireland amid the foulest enemies of the Dragon Kings—the Dark Fae.

The Dark were set on capturing a Dragon King. Recently, they had managed to hold two—Kellan and Tristan—for a short period before both escaped. Though it had been a close call, especially with Kellan.

Each time it had been narrow escapes. The Dragon Kings and their friends hadn't escaped unscathed. There were injuries, but the worst was that Rhi had been taken by the Dark.

Rhi. Kiril couldn't help but grin as he thought of the Light Fae. Though the Kings had waged war on both sides of the Fae, Rhi was different. For a time, she had been the lover of a Dragon King.

And no King would ever forget that.

None of them really understood what tore Rhi and her lover apart, and they likely never would. He never spoke of her, never mentioned her name. And Rhi . . . had returned to the Light to take up her duties. Oddly enough, it was her interference in telling a Warrior that he was half-Fae and her prince that brought her back into the fold of the Kings.

She hadn't been thrilled about it, and had, in fact, told them all where to go. Yet, when trouble came, it was Rhi who rushed in to save Kellan and his mate, Denae. Then she did it again with Tristan and Sammi—to Rhi's peril.

Kiril was determined to locate where the Dark were holding Rhi. It was one of the many things he was going to ascertain while spying. Every minute of every day brought him closer to danger. Returning time and again to the Dark's pub, *an Doras,* only quickened the inevitable.

Not that a Dragon King ever shied from danger.

It was all worth it if he could rescue Rhi and learn who was out to reveal them to the world. The fact their faceless enemy aligned themselves with the Dark Fae as well as MI5 meant that they were prepared to do anything.

And so was Kiril. He would give himself up to

the Dark before he allowed anything to happen to his brothers. It just might come to that too.

The Dark knew who he was, had known for days. It was a game they played with each other. He pretended not to know they watched the home he bought, and they were never far from wherever he was while they pretended that they had no idea he was a Dragon King.

He had to guard his every word, mind his every move. It was exhausting. And exhilarating. It had been ages since he'd had such an opponent. In the end, however, he had to remember it wasn't a game. Their competition would decide who got to remain on the realm—the Dark or the Kings.

Not once since he came to Ireland had Kiril dared to take to the skies—even in a rainstorm. The urge to shift into a dragon and have the air rush over his scales and along his wings was irresistible, crushing.

He gripped the steering wheel and gradually took control of himself. He slowed the car as he drew closer to Cork. Cork, like Venice, was built on the water with the city center situated on an island in the River Lee, upstream from Cork Harbor. With the River Lee separating into two branches and surrounding the city center, there were numerous bridges giving Cork a distinctive look and feel.

The city was pretty, but it wasn't home. Kiril longed for Scotland and Dreagan. He came to a stop at an intersection and waited for the light to turn green. The Shandon Bells of the eighteenth-century Church of St. Anne suddenly filled the air. The old-world style of Cork only made him miss Scotland all the more, but most especially Dreagan and the mountains that were home.

The sixty thousand acres of Dreagan were a haven for the Dragon Kings. With restricted air space over their land, they could shift and fly whenever they wanted. The fact Dreagan whisky was the finest in the world kept them in luxury. Every restaurant and pub sought to sell Dreagan, but they were selective in who they allowed to sell their whisky. The Irish whisky he sampled while in Ireland was passable, but what he wouldn't do for a bottle of Dreagan.

Kiril found a parking space and quickly pulled the Mercedes in before he cut the engine. He didn't plan on being in the city long, but the dark clouds hinted at rain. Kiril closed the roof with a simple press of a button and stepped out of the car.

He fastened the first button of his suit jacket and glanced around to see how many were watching. Three Dark were visible and doing a poor job of trying to blend in. Kiril imagined there were at least four more watching him as they did on previous nights.

"Here we go again," he mumbled to himself and locked the car before he strode to the sidewalk.

Every time he came to Cork it was for show. He ate at expensive restaurants—sometimes alone, sometimes with different women. He visited different pubs, but always he returned to *an Doras* before heading home.

Occasionally alone, and at times with women.

Kiril had one hand in the pocket of his slacks when his gaze snagged on a pair of legs that seemed to go on for miles. Her black skirt skimmed high up on her thighs, and her platform heels only made those shapely limbs appear longer.

He paused and let his gaze wander up her legs to the curve of her hips. A silver shirt sparkled with sequins at the hem banded around her, accentuating her trim waist. The shirt was loose, flowing while the back crisscrossed in a large X showing a wealth of creamy skin. Her black hair was pulled to the side in a messy braid that fell over her left shoulder. She kept her back to him as she peered in the window of a shop.

Her eyes lifted and locked with his through the window. He was thoroughly mesmerized. Awestruck.

Entranced.

Her beauty left him speechless, dumbstruck. His gaze was riveted on her. Kiril took a step toward her when she turned to face him.

His lungs locked, the air trapped as he gazed upon loveliness unlike any he had ever encountered. Her oval face was utter perfection. Thin black brows arched over large silver eyes. Her cheekbones were impossibly high and tinted with a hint of blush. Her lips, full and wide, made his balls tighten and his cock ache.

She was Fae, but not even that made him turn away. Kiril had encountered many beautiful Fae, yet there was something entirely different about this one. He blinked, and that's when he saw her glamour shift. If he hadn't been so enamored, he would have spotted it sooner.

Disappointment filled him when he noticed the thick strip of silver hair against her cheek and her red eyes signaling she was Dark Fae.

It didn't take much for him to deduce that the Dark wanted to use her against him. It was a good thing he could see through glamour, or he might really have found himself in a pickle.

He should walk away, but he couldn't. Nor did he want to. He wanted to know the female, and by getting close to her she might let something slip that could help him in his quest.

His game just became infinitely more dangerous, and yet, there was a small thrill that made his stomach tighten at the idea of learning more about the Dark. She was thoroughly intoxicating to look at, and if the intelligence he spotted shining through her eyes was any indication, she was going to completely fascinate him.

Thank you for reading **Wild Need**. I hope you enjoyed it! If you liked this book – or any of my other releases – please consider rating the book at the online retailer of your choice. Your ratings and reviews help other readers find new favorites, and of course there is no better or more appreciated support for an author than word of mouth recommendations from happy readers. Thanks again for your interest in my books!

Donna Grant

www.DonnaGrant.com

ABOUT THE AUTHOR

New York Times and *USA Today* bestselling author Donna Grant has been praised for her "totally addictive" and "unique and sensual" stories. She's written more than thirty novels spanning multiple genres of romance including the bestselling Dark King series featuring immortal Highlander shape shifting dragons who are daring, untamed, and seductive. She lives with her husband, two children, a dog, and four cats in Texas.

Connect online at:

www.DonnaGrant.com

www.facebook.com/AuthorDonnaGrant

www.twitter.com/donna_grant

www.goodreads.com/donna_grant/

Never miss a new book
From Donna Grant!

Sign up for Donna's email newsletter at
www.DonnaGrant.com

Be the first to get notified of new releases and be eligible for special subscribers-only exclusive content and giveaways. Sign up today!

43914590R00134

Made in the USA
San Bernardino, CA
04 January 2017